I'm Doin' Me

I'm Doin' Me

Anna Black

www.urbanbooks.net

Urban Books, LLC
97 N 18th Street
Wyandanch, NY 11798

ISBN 13: 978-1-62286-752-3
ISBN 10: 1-62286-752-1

First Mass Market Printing November 2016
First Trade Paperback Printing January 2015
Printed in the United States of America

10 9 8 7 6 5 4 3 2 1

Distributed by Kensington Publishing Corp.
Submit Orders to:
Customer Service
400 Hahn Road
Westminster, MD 21157-4627
Phone: 1-800-733-3000
Fax: 1-800-659-2436

I'm Doin' Me

Anna Black

Also by Anna Black

Now You Wanna Come Back
Luck of the Draw
Who Do I Run To?
Now You Wanna Come Back 2
Who Do I Run To Now?
Now You Wanna Come Back 3
Split Image
If It Wasn't For Tony
Mr. Wrong
I Just Wanna Be Loved
Hooks In Me
A Special Holiday
The Illest Na Na

Chapter One

Tiffany sat at her desk waiting for the morning circus to begin. She was the executive producer for a hit television show called *Boy Crazy*, and she knew that the next season could be the last because the young ladies' characters on the show would be graduating high school and going to college. Whether or not they would continue the series was still up in the air. She hated the waiting game. Her idea was to allow the characters to bypass college and become young adults, starting their new life adventures, trying to find their way in life with episodes about job hunting, moving out of their parents' pool houses, and starting new careers—things that most recent well-off graduates do. Since the women were not the teens they portrayed on the show, she wanted to turn their characters into young adults, not college girls. They were now in their early twenties, and one cast member, Joy, was starting to look it.

She tapped her pencil on her desk, not able to concentrate because the thought of losing her show made her feel sick. She hadn't felt that kind of fear in her gut in a while. She nervously went over the details of her proposal for the show a million times, hoping that the legendary *Boy Crazy* would continue. At five minutes 'til ten, she stood and grabbed her files and notes. "Meeting time," she said to herself.

She hurried out of her office to get to the meeting, but her assistant, Myah, greeted her with a bright smile. "Okay, boss lady, you know what to do. Go in there and claim your new concept."

"I will try. Since Bill has been gone, things have been so different. It is going to be difficult getting my ideas across to his pompous asshole of a brother. You know he wanted to cut our show first, even though it's the number one show on this network."

Myah brushed lint from Tiffany's shoulder. "Because it's a black show and you know our shows get, what, seven seasons tops?"

"Yeah, but I came in and saved this show," Tiffany said. "And I'm not about to walk away without a fight. We have won several awards the last three years and rumor has it we have more coming this year, so he'd better not say no."

Myah nodded.

Tiffany had lucked up on her job. She had gone to school for broadcasting and hoped to be a show host or anchorwoman someday, but landed a job purely by accident as a screenwriter and then later, as an executive producer. She was in the right place at the right time, she said every time she was asked how she got started.

She'd never forget that day. She had an interview to become a broadcaster for an online news segment, on KCLN's Web site, a cable network that competed with popular stations like UPN and TBS. She walked in and asked directions to where she needed to be. With directions in her mental Rolodex, she went to the right floor, but walked through the wrong door. It was a meeting of screenwriters for *Boy Crazy*. When she walked in, the producer of the show, Todd, assumed she was the new writer.

"Great, you're here. Have a seat," he instructed. When she did, he continued. "Now, we are going into our new season. I need ideas, and I need them now!" He spoke like a man unmistakably in charge. "We know that Shana is now with our new cast member, Chase, and he is slime, the worst of the worst, and he only has sex on his little menacing mind. Who do you think we should allow him to hit on behind Shana's back, Claire or Joy?"

Tiffany spoke up first. She was familiar with the show because she watched it faithfully, and she wanted to impress him since she thought this was her interview. "I say Claire. She is not likely to be trusted since she has had a history of dating both of their ex-boyfriends. Her confession about Chase will come across as vindictive, and when Shana doesn't believe her, Claire sets up Chase with her Web cam to prove to Shana that she is telling the truth. That brings the girls a bit closer to seeing that Claire is not the horrible person she reflects on the outside."

The producer agreed. "And what should we do about Claire's mother deciding to divorce her dad because she thinks he had the affair with Claire's dance teacher?" he asked.

Tiffany jumped in again before anyone else. "We know that the encounter at the restaurant was innocent. I think Claire should intervene and go on a so-called investigation of her own to get to the truth to convince her mom to stay. That will give her and her friends a quest to join forces to save her parents' marriage."

"Brilliant," he said. "I suggest you guys put your heads together and come up with something extravagant for the upcoming season. And you, new girl, are impressive. Welcome to the team." He shook Tiffany's hand and she

smiled. She didn't know the job was for a writer for her favorite show.

Seconds later, the actual new girl walked in. "I'm so sorry I'm late. Traffic was crazy," she said and put her bag down. Her natural curls were wild around her milk chocolate face, and she seemed to be out of breath.

"Who are you?" Todd asked.

"I'm Tracy, your new writer," she said and extended her hand.

"If she's Tracy, who are you?" he asked Tiffany.

"I'm Tiffany Richardson. I am here for the broadcasting position."

"Well, Tiffany, broadcasting is not your calling. And you, Tracy, are late, so you lose." He got up and exited the room.

Tracy looked at Tiffany with a look of total confusion. She looked around, hoping someone would say something, but everyone gathered their things to leave the room.

"Are you serious? This has to be a joke right?" Tracy said, blinking almost one hundred times a second.

"Yes, ma'am. You missed your chance, Miss Tardiness," Darryl, another writer, said. Everyone began to leave the room.

"Son of a bitch!" Tracy yelled.

"Look, I'm sorry," Tiffany said. "I walked in thinking it was an interview for the broadcasting spot," she tried to explained.

Tracy shook her head. "I don't give a shit. I have worked my entire life to get here, and now it's being snatched from under me by someone who doesn't even qualify for the job? This won't be the last time you or KCLN hears from me. I'll be calling my lawyer!" She stormed out.

Tiffany sat and tried to take in what just happened. Unsure where to go or what to do next, she decided to find Todd and ask him what's next. She asked around and finally made it to his office.

"Come in," he yelled when she tapped on the door.

Walking in slowly, she said, "Listen, Todd, I don't have a clue where to go from here. I mean, I came in for a different position and you mistook me for Tracy. I don't want to take anyone's job," she protested.

"You're not taking anything, I'm giving it to you," he said and stood. "Come follow me."

She complied.

They went down the hall and stopped at a door with the name TRACY SIMMS on it. Todd slid the nameplate out and opened the door. "This will be your office or what I like to call *your thinking chamber. There is a comfy sofa for you to lay back and let your imagination take you anywhere that results in a successful show."*

Tiffany looked around in amazement. She didn't expect anything as lovely as this office and she thought she'd burst.

"Now," he continued, "take this down to the personnel office and they will get you processed. Be back in the morning at nine sharp, ready to work with your team to write thirty fun and crazy episodes for next season."

"I thought each season was only twenty-two episodes," she said.

"Yes, but we write thirty because some are not worth airing," he said and walked out.

She found her way to the HR department and sat down to fill out her paperwork. Her eyes bulged when she saw her contract and her new salary.

"Ma'am, is this correct?" she asked.

"Yes, ma'am. You get this per episode," the rep said.

Looking at all the zeroes made Tiffany dizzy. "I need a glass of water," she said.

The older, thin, gray-haired woman got up and got her some water from a cooler in the corner of the office. "You're the first writer to act this surprised," she said, handing Tiffany a paper cup. "I've been here for twenty-four years, and they always want more," she joked.

"Well, I came here for a job making five times less than this," Tiffany said.

"Well, Boy Crazy is like the fifth or sixth show for this network in ranking, and it has only been on the air for one season."

Tiffany took a deep breath, worried that she may have gotten in way over her head. She finished signing all the documents and headed out, anxious to call her mother. In the car, she dialed her and filled her in on the miracle that just happened. She went home, excited to tell her roommate that she'd be finding a new place in thirty days. The money she'd be making called for a more upscale type of living arrangement. Making that much, she could now afford to buy a new set of wheels, too.

"Asia!" she called when she walked in. "Asia!" she yelled again when there was no reply. "You will never guess what happened to me today."

Her roommate finally came out of her room. She had on a robe, a clear indication that she was maybe in the middle of or just finishing up some grown folks' business. "Shhhhh," she instructed with a finger over her lips.

Tiffany lowered her voice. "I'm sorry. I didn't know you were entertaining. I've got some news that will blow your mind."

"What, girl? What?"

Tiffany grabbed a wine glass and poured it half full of Merlot and took a sip before she continued. "You will never believe what happened to me today." She grinned.

"Okay aw'redee, wat in da bumbaclot hap'-pon?" Asia asked, lapsing into her Jamaica, dialect.

"I went to KCLN for that broadcasting gig, but ended up getting a job as a writer for Boy Crazy," Tiffany squealed.

"Waddddd? Yah lie," her friend snapped back.

"No, mi no lie," Tiffany said, trying to imitate her.

"Oh my God, Tiff, that is, like, amazing," Now Asia sounded like the sixth-grade schoolteacher she was. Not the Jamaican sister who grew up in Brooklyn.

"Yes, and this is my thirty-day notice. I am moving out. I am going to be making more than I made in the last six months in just one episode. I can't believe that it just happened like that." Tiffany snapped her fingers for emphasis.

"Wow, Tiff. That is incredible. I am so happy for you," Asia said, hugging her tight.

"Thanks so much, Asia, and I promise when I am settled and things are normal, I will pay you back for all that you have done for me."

Asia put her hands up and shook her head. "Tiff, come on. When you moved in, I told you that I wanted to help. Help means help, and you, my sista, don't owe me a ting."

Tiffany hugged her even tighter. "Thank you so much, Asia. You are like an angel. God put you in the right place at the right time. If it weren't for you, I would have been on the streets," she exclaimed. "Moving from Chicago to pursue my dream was one thing. Getting here and finding out the beachfront property I signed a lease online with was a crack house wasn't the worst thing to happen to me. Not getting my two grand back for the deposit was," she said and they laughed.

"Well, if you hadda changed your clothes the next morning instead of having on the same outfit that you had on the morning before, I would have never known that you were in need of a little assistance." Asia went to light the fire under the tea kettle.

"I know, right? I slept in the diner that night. I was grateful that Miss Alma didn't make me leave." Tiffany shook her head, thinking back.

"Well, it worked out for us both."

"I don't know how you drink that. Tea is so awful." Tiffany frowned, watching her roommate get tea out of the cupboard. She took a swallow of her Merlot and took a seat.

"Tea is not awful. It's better than all the wine ya' drink. Boy, I swear, you Yankee gals."

"Hey, you said you wouldn't call me that."

"Yes, you're right, mi sor'ey."

Her lover came out of her room "Baby, mi gon' push off," he said. Asia went over and wrapped her arms around his neck.

"Will mi see ya later?" she asked.

"Of course," he said and kissed her. She watched him walk out the door.

"My goodness, Asia," Tiffany said. "Where do you find these fine-ass men? I mean, for crying out loud, you're a schoolteacher."

"Hey, what I do in the daytime is one thing, and what I do at night is another."

Tiffany laughed. She grabbed her wine and headed to her room and looked around. She was happy to know that she finally would be able to afford a place of her own and not have to live in this eight-by-eight box anymore. She still slept on a twin-sized bed because nothing else fit. She hadn't totally unpacked because there was no storage in her little room, but she was grateful she wasn't homeless.

That was episodes ago. Now she was established and doing well as the executive producer and head writer for *Boy Crazy*. Today was the day she had to convince Todd and the evil-ass, non-smiling bastard, and acting CEO that the show needed to transition from high school graduation to college graduation. She felt the show did not have to pick up with the girls being in college, because every situation they could get into had already been done in all the episodes of them being "boy crazy" in high school.

"Myah, please promise me that you will be on my team even if it's not at KCLN," she asked. Her assistant was the best of the best when it came to assistants.

"If that means I won't be on the unemployment line, I'll promise," Myah said.

Finally, it was time for Tiffany to walk into the idea room. That was where they sat at a large oval table to play with their ideas. "I can't promise you that just yet, but I know my life would be an unorganized mess without you."

"Well, go in there and keep us both employed," Myah said, giving her boss a little shove.

Tiffany went in and took her seat. Todd walked in with Mr. Keiffer. Mr. Keiffer was the network owner's brother. He was filling in because Bill, the real deal, was out ill. His presence in the room made a difference. Tiffany's confidence deserted her. For the first time in the idea room, she was fresh out of ideas.

Chapter Two

Tiffany said, "I think the show has run its course with these women playing students. Shana is almost twenty-four, and the cameras are not so agreeable to Joy anymore. She doesn't look seventeen anymore. I think the new season should be about their lives after college graduation. We can then focus on the ladies coming into adulthood. You know, like starting their lives, looking for husbands, planning for children, getting a mortgage, and so forth; grown folk's stuff. The show will be like a new-age *Girlfriends* or *Sex and the City*."

The approval on Todd's face was in contrast to the disapproval on Mr. Keiffer's face. "Miss Richardson," he said, "that's the point. I don't want this show to shout *Girlfriends* or *Sex and the City*."

"It won't, sir. That is just the foundation of the show. Trust me, women eighteen to fifty are going to love this show. It is going to be a newer version of those series that women loved, but with a fresh appeal. With all due respect, William gave me creative rights over this show before he became ill. He put this show in my hands, Mr. Keiffer, and technically I have the right to take the show in whatever direction I choose."

Mr. Keiffer didn't budge. "And this is still my network, Miss Richardson, and I decide what shows stays or goes." He leaned toward Todd, whispered something into his ear, and then stood. He walked out with no more words to Tiffany, just a nod to Todd with a look that said, "Handle this."

"Come up with college material," Todd said as soon as the door shut behind Mr. Keiffer.

"Come on, Todd," Tiffany said. "These three characters are close, but in some cases, best buds attend different schools. To put all three girls in the same college won't be realistic and we are going to lose our audience. Hell, Joy looks like she is going on thirty."

Even though Mr. Keiffer was intimidating, her team nodded in agreement, and Darryl said, "So true," loud enough for the room to hear him.

"Come up with a college storyline or there's no more show," Todd said firmly.

"Todd, you can't be serious," Tiffany protested in disbelief. He'd always had her back, and she wondered why Mr. Keiffer forced him to put his tail between his legs.

"I'm dead serious. Listen, Tiff, I wanna back you on this, but this is above my head," he said.

She couldn't believe the words coming out of his mouth. He'd always given her complete creative control.

"Todd, you gotta talk to him," she cried desperately.

"Come on, Tiff, you've pulled us from number six to number one in just one season, so come up with something fabulous like you always do." He walked out, leaving her speechless.

"Now what?" Darryl, her coexecutive producer, asked.

Tiffany had no idea. Her hopes of turning her *Boy Crazy* cast into adults and not crazy college students had just been shot down. "I don't know," she admitted for the first time. All the writers on her team sat in silence. "Okay let's take a vote, and I want everyone at this table to be one hundred percent honest with me." She knew they would be. If an episode idea was corny, they'd make it known. And as a team, they would make it right. "All in favor of college days for *Boy Crazy,* raise your hand."

Only one of the six hands went up. *I knew your white ass would be,* she thought, looking at Brad. He was the only non-black writer for the show. "All in favor for post college raise your hand," she said. The other five writers raised their hands.

"Okay, no worries, you guys," she declared. "*Boy Crazy* must go on, but it may not be with KCLN."

After she got back to her desk, she wished she could take back her words. "Oh my God," she cried. "What am I going to do? If I don't get another season, I and several others will not have a job." Her intercom buzzed. "Yes, Myah?"

"Your cast members are here."

"Please send them in." All three walked in seconds later. "Ladies, how are you?"

Melinda spoke up first. "Not good, girl. Rumor has it that the network won't give us another season after this senior year season."

"Yes, that is true, not a rumor. That's only if we bypass college. I know you ladies are tired of being students. We've had this conversation many times before. If we don't do what the network wants, I need to know your opinions on where we should go from here," Tiffany said nervously.

Tia shook her head. "Go from here? Tiffany, if there is no more show after this season, where else can we go?"

"To another network," she said. The women looked confused. "Listen, I was thinking I should start shopping the show to other networks, but it's more effective if the original cast members are on board. I have to get a commitment from you ladies that if KCLN doesn't sign us for another term, then we are willing to go to another network. Bill trusted me, and I know he didn't leave me in charge of this hit show for his arrogant-ass brother to shut it down. If he wants to shut it down here, he can, but we can take it to another network." Tiffany studied the three women sitting before her.

The ladies looked at each other.

"Well, I'm in," Melinda agreed.

Tia then agreed. "Yes, if you can keep the show running."

The only one left to say she was in was Jennifer. "I don't know, Tiffany," she said. "I mean, how hard will it be to get us a new home? I would love for the show to go on, but if it's not, I have to keep my options open. I don't need to be off the scene too long. That would be murder to my career."

"I know, Jennifer," Tiffany said. "But we have an entire season ahead of us, and that gives me a little time to at least shop the show. It wouldn't be the same without you."

"Okay, okay, okay," Jennifer relented. "I'm in. Hell, this show was my start to fame, and if I can play Claire for another ten years and be adored by my fans, I'm in."

"Great, ladies, that is great. I will be honest, I have one more meeting with the heads, and if they are not saying anything, this season, while we are taping, I will do my best to shop the show. Hopefully, get us another network that wants to do what we want to do."

"Well, Tiff, I trust you, but be sure that Claire has the hottest crib and ride in our adult series," Jennifer said.

"Hey, I want a nice crib too," Tia said.

"Listen, ladies, those are small details. We have to find a home first. If KCLN doesn't want us, we will find a network that does. Hell, our show is number one on this network. They will yield," Tiffany said with confidence.

A week later, after impatiently waiting for the verdict from Mr. Keiffer, Tiffany got the sad news from Todd that the network would not yield.

They wanted what they wanted, even though the writers and the cast members thought otherwise.

She left the office for the first time pissed off and beyond confused. She never saw the show coming to an end, but that was exactly what was going to happen after the taping of this season. She felt like a Mack Truck hit her in her chest. Not wanting to stick around after hearing the news, she left early and drove home in a daze, wondering how she was going to deliver on her promise to her writers and cast members to find another network. She had no leads and no idea how she was going to start to shop the show.

She pulled into her driveway and smiled a little when she saw Jeff's car. Her boyfriend was at her place a little more than she cared for, but she didn't complain because at least he did cook. She walked in, tossed her keys into the bowl on the table near the door, and stepped out of her shoes. On the way to the fridge after grabbing a wine glass, she thought she heard a giggle. She paused and listened, but heard nothing. She proceeded to get the wine from the fridge and could have sworn she heard moaning. She stopped again to listen. The sounds got louder.

"Awww, hell naw," she mumbled and put the wine bottle and glass on the counter. She made her way to her bedroom and pushed the door open to find Jeff in bed with her housekeeper, Carmen.

The other woman's toes were pointed to the ceiling while Jeff's toned ass rolled around deep inside her pussy. The scent of sex was in the air, and from the way the bed was in disarray, Tiffany could tell they had been at it for a little while.

"Get the fuck outta my damn bed!" she roared. The couple jumped up. "Are you fucking kidding me, Jeff?" she yelled even louder. "I mean, for real?"

The maid got up, scrambled for her dress, and quickly stepped into it, but Jeff sat on the side of the bed.

"Miss Richardson, I am so sorry," she said with her thick Spanish accent.

She was sexy, young, and stupid, Tiffany thought, wondering why she even attempted to offer an apology.

"I am so, so sorry," she said again.

Tiffany addressed her without taking her eyes off Jeff. "Get out, Carmen, you are fired! Don't ever step foot in my house again!"

The woman tried to make a quick exit, but she didn't move past Tiffany fast enough. With a thrust of her foot, Tiffany shoved her out the door.

"What don't I do, Jeff, huh? Tell me what the fuck do I not do? I suck your dick. I fuck you in the strangest places because that turns you on. I pay my own damn mortgage and bills and I don't ask you for shit. All I ask of you is to be my fucking boyfriend, and for that you decide to fuck another woman in my bed?"

His answer was said so low she barely heard him.

"What? Excuse me?" she asked. She wanted him to be a man and say what the fuck he had to say.

"I can't compete," he said, this time speaking louder.

"Compete? Compete, Jeffrey?" Tiffany was confused. "What the hell do you mean? What do you mean by that?"

"You . . . you are this gorgeous, popular executive producer and writer for the hottest show on television. You are invited to exclusive parties, red carpet events, and movie premiers. All I do is fix cars. It's like I'm just your date or your escort, not your man or your boyfriend," he said.

She wanted to slap the shit out of him. "Jeff, you cannot be serious. Every event, every party, and every red carpet event, you are there. Every magazine or captured moment is with your ass."

"But the focus is on you!" he yelled.

For a moment, Tiffany felt as if the wind had been knocked out of her. When she caught her breath, she got in touch with her anger. She truly wanted to punch him in the face.

"That is because of what I do, Jeff. The focus would be on you if we attended a red carpet mechanics event. When I met you, I met you as the guy who fixed my Beemer, and when you asked me out, did I ever once throw me all up in your face? When I told you at the table that night on our first date what I did and who I was, you said you could handle it. Never did I make you feel like less of a man. If you felt that way, that was your own personal issues, so don't blame it on me.

"The thing is, right now, I'm not even mad at you for fucking around on me. No, that is not what I'm mad about. I am mad as hell at the fact that you thought it was okay to fuck her in my damn bed. You had the audacity to go there with her here, in my room, in my bed, on my fucking satin sheets. You should have fucked that bitch in the guest room on the cotton ones if your dick needed to be pleased that bad!"

"You are right," he said. He finally stood, and she saw he still had an erection. She wondered briefly how his dick was still hard after he had just gotten busted.

"Make sure you get all of your things and give me my key before you leave," she said and stormed off to the kitchen. She grabbed the wine bottle and instead of pouring a glass, she put the bottle up to her lips and took a long swig. Her eyes burned, but she refused to cry. "You are not going to be defeated, Tiffany Lashaye Richardson. Don't you shed one tear for that bastard," she coached herself and took another swig.

The bottle was almost finished by the time Jeff came out with his duffle bag. "Well, I got everything," he said.

Tiffany didn't look at him. "My key, please?" He tossed it and she caught it. "See your way out, and please don't even attempt to dial my number again."

Jeff didn't argue, he just left. When she heard the door close, she broke down. Her career and love life were in the toilet in the space of a few hours, and she didn't know how she was going to bounce back.

Chapter Three

The next day, Tiffany sat in her office and watched the clock. She tried to avoid thoughts of Jeff and the events that had taken place the day before, but couldn't. She knew it was best to talk about it, but she was too busy pretending it never happened.

Work was the best thing for her to keep her mind occupied. She'd thought that working on writing the final season of *Boy Crazy* would be enough to take her mind off things, but it wasn't. She tried to focus, but she couldn't help but think of Jeff. He was the perfect boyfriend, she thought at times, because they never argued. He gave her space, and she gave him his. The sex was fantastic, and the brother could hang a suit. The gossip in L.A. was he was her frog prince because after they hooked up, he cleaned up. He owned an auto shop that wasn't the shop to go to until Tiffany turned all of her friends on to it. Even though his business grew rapidly, he never felt accomplished enough and she couldn't understand why.

He was Idris Elba fine, with cocoa skin and a body that would not offend society if he walked around naked. He wasn't a big romantic, but there were moments when he made Tiffany feel like she was a queen. She wasn't the average L.A. woman, meaning she was on the opposite end of a size zero. She was a Chicagoan and most women looked like her back home. They were considered thick, not fat, like L.A. natives saw her.

She was a twelve on a good day and her body was curvy. Her breasts still stood up, and her stomach wasn't bigger than her ass, so she looked sexy in everything she wore. Not light bright, but golden honey complexioned with relaxed hair that hung a little past her shoulders, she was sassy, and she turned heads. Being smart and on top of her game made her a catch. As far as she was concerned, Jeff had messed up the best thing he'd ever have. She was just going to have to get over it, she told herself. She grabbed her notes and eased by Myah to head to the idea room.

Today she didn't feel as passionate about her job as she had been the years before. How was she going to save her cast's and crew's jobs?

Her thoughts jogged up and down her mind escalator, but she shut the power off when she walked into the idea room.

"Okay, ladies and gents," she said as she took a seat. "We have to write a slamming season, and it has to be hot enough to get us another gig with another network or make KCLN change their minds. When I point to you, I want to hear some good shit. It's the girls' senior year, and we need some excitement, something suspenseful, and humorous. This is our moment, guys, so we gotta hit it." She opened her portfolio to a blank page. "Norma, you're up. Go."

"Claire confesses she's a virgin."

Tiffany jotted it down. "Darryl," she called out, without looking up from her notebook.

"Joy finds out her parents are secretly separated."

"Brad."

"The girls freak out about taking the SATs for college," he said.

"Shelby."

After five hours of going at it, they had the first few episode ideas mapped out. Tiffany decided it was time for a break, so she let everyone leave. Instead of eating the same old tuna sandwich from their cafeteria, she decided she'd go out for lunch. She decided on a little outdoor restaurant

not far from her office building. After sitting
down and ordering pasta salad, she looked
around. A guy two tables over looked familiar to
her, and only after a few seconds of ogling, it hit
her.

"Kory," she said loud enough for him to hear.

He looked her way. "Yes?" he replied.

"Kory Banks, right?"

"Yes, from KBanks Jewelers."

"No, CVS high school, in Chicago."

"Awww, snap. Tiffany Richardson, right?"

"Yes, it's me," she replied.

He got up and walked over to her table. They
exchanged a quick hug and began to catch up.
They got past, "What brought you to L.A.?" and
what they were doing now with their lives.

The waitress brought Tiffany's order and she
asked Kory to join her. He grabbed his cold sandwich and took a seat. They continued talking,
neither one of them eating until Tiffany realized
she had to get back to the office.

"Wow, Tiffany Richardson. Wait 'til I tell
Kennedy I ran into you," he said.

Tiffany recognized the name. Kennedy was
Kory's younger cousin. The two girls had been
good friends in high school. They had both graduated the year after Kory. "Wow, Kennedy," she
said. "How is she?"

"She is good, running her very own jewelry store back home."

"Man, that is awesome," she said. She looked at her watch. "Listen, Kory, here is my card. My cell is on it. Please give me a buzz and we can possibly grab dinner or something."

Kory gave her his card too. "Great. And it was good seeing you, Tiff. I mean, you look incredible."

"And so do you. L.A. has certainly treated you well."

"Yes, it has," he said.

They said their good-byes and she hurried back to her building. When she walked into the idea room, everyone got quiet.

"I'm going to assume we got some writing done in my absence?" she asked. A few moments later, she learned that they actually had been working and had some fantastic ideas.

They finished out the day and everybody went home. Tiffany couldn't wait to call her homegirl back in Chicago, Rose, to tell her about running into Kory.

"No way, not Kory Banks," she said, sounding shocked.

"Yes, girl. There I was, sitting there after ordering my pasta salad and I noticed him sitting two tables over."

"Small world for real. I know you got his number?" Rose asked.

"Fo'sho. You know I had the biggest crush on Kory in school," Tiffany said as she grabbed her Bailey's ice cream from the freezer.

"Crush is an understatement. You were obsessed with him."

"I was not," Tiffany protested.

"Yes, Tiff, you were. I remember you'd stay at your locker until after he walked away sometimes, even if it made you late for class."

"Yes, I guess I was cuckoo for Kory back then."

"And now?"

"Girl, I don't know what I feel. It's like . . . seeing him was like laying my eyes on an angel. And you know, after what happened to me yesterday with Jeff, I thought God sent Kory in to save the day."

"Maybe he did," Rose said.

"I don't know. I mean, we caught up, but he didn't look at me with that 'oooh, I'm happy to see you' look. You know, there was no flirting."

"Well, the next step is to call him. You're a grown-ass woman now. You don't have to have a secret crush anymore."

"Yes, you're right," Tiffany said, looking at his card. "Listen, I will wait 'til tomorrow. Give him a call and see when he is free, and if I find out he is single, I will make my move."

"Well, you'd better keep me posted. I want to know all the details."

"I know you do and don't go telling your nosey-ass sister, Rose. I'm serious, she talks too much."

"Okay, I won't say a word."

They got off the phone and Tiffany went to shower. She got into bed and turned on the tube. Her phone vibrated. A text from Jeff:

I'm sorry. Didn't mean to hurt you.

She deleted it and got comfortable in bed. A couple moments later, she got another text from him:

Can I come over?

She sent a text back with a one word reply:

No.

The next text she got said he just wanted to talk. She sighed and typed a longer reply:

Stop textin me, I don't wanna C U or TTY!

He continued to text her for another hour. Finally tired of hearing the notifications going off, she put her phone on silent so she could get some sleep.

Chapter Four

Day two of writing was exhausting, and Tiffany couldn't wait to call it quits. She headed back to her office and stopped by Myah's desk to see if anyone had returned any of her calls. No one had. She'd called every network in the book, trying to get an appointment, but kept getting the same "I'll have someone call you back" response.

Frustrated and tired, she sat at her desk and kicked off her shoes. She undid her suit jacket and then opened her right bottom drawer and pulled out her bottle of Remy. It was her pick-me-up on days like this, when she needed a hug. She grabbed her empty coffee mug and poured some in and took a sip.

"God help me," she said out loud. Her line rang. "Yes, Myah?" Her assistant announced that someone was on the line from UVN, Urban Views Network, a place where Tiffany knew the show would continue to be a success. "Hi, this is Tiffany," she said when the call was patched through.

"Hey, Tiffany, this is Amanda. How are you today?"

"I'm great, Amanda. It is so good to hear from you."

"Likewise. What's going on, Tiffany? What can I do you for?"

"Well, as you know, *Boy Crazy* is going into its final season," she explained. "KCLN is not on board with some of the producers, writers, and cast members' ideas and they may not give us a new contract." She hoped to hear positive news over the phone, but she ended up being transferred to Amanda's assistant to set up an appointment. Which was fine after she thought about it; at least she had made one contact.

She was shocked by the lack of response she was getting. *Boy Crazy* was such a brilliant show, and she just wanted somebody to give them a break. She made a few more phone calls and then decided she'd call it a day.

Now that work was left at the office, Kory was the first thing that jumped into her mind when she got in the car. She fished for his card and called him before pulling out of her parking space.

"This is Kory," he answered.

"Hi, Kory, this is Tiffany. How are you?"

"I'm great, Tiffany, how are you?"

"Good," she said. Then it was dead silence. That was bad. "I, ummm, just wanted to touch base with you and see if you were free for dinner." Nervous, she hoped he wouldn't say no.

"Well, tonight I'm not, but tomorrow is good for me," he said.

She accepted. That was only one day. She had gone without seeing her high school love for years, so twenty-four hours would be a piece a cake she thought. "Sure, tomorrow would be perfect. There is a Fig & Olive on Melrose, say around seven?" she asked and hoped that would be acceptable.

"I'm familiar. That will be great."

She smiled. "Cool, I look forward to seeing you."

"You too, Tiff, take care."

They hung up. She scrolled through her numbers until she got to Rose's name. She wanted to call her before she called Asia. She wanted to go by Asia's to see Asia in person and fill her in on the details about Kory because she had never mentioned him to her before. To run into him in L.A. was mind-blowing. She couldn't wait to tell her friend the entire history of her high school crush.

She squealed when Rose answered, "Okay, he agreed to meet me for dinner tomorrow."

"Tiff, that is like the best news I've heard all week. I mean, like, are you going to tell him that you were in love from the first moment you saw him?"

"Ummm, no," Tiffany said and laughed.

"Why not?"

"Because that sounds corny and juvenile, Rose. I can't come off like a stalker."

"Yeah, you're right, that may come off a little too strong."

"Yes, I am going to take my time, play it cool, and then I am going to devour him," Tiffany joked.

"Oooh, girl, you so nasty," Rose said playfully.

"Yes, I am. I feel like a horny teenager, Rose, just thinking about it. God, I loved me some Kory back then."

"What about now?"

"Rose, come on, be serious. I like him. He's still sexy as hell, but I don't know that man. He could be a beater, or weird, you know, like have some crazy-ass foot fetish or worse." Tiffany paused, and they both said, "Gay," and burst into laughter. "Oh Lord, Rose, if he is gay, I may slit my wrist," she joked.

"Well, you said he was dressed nice, and you do live out in L.A. A bus ride from San Francisco," she joked.

Tiffany didn't like that one bit. "Shut up, Rose, don't jinx it. I am so sure he isn't gay, okay? And we will never say that about my future husband and baby daddy again. Understood?" She cranked the engine, because she was starting to sweat in her hot-ass car.

"Understood," Rose said.

The two women got off the phone and Tiffany went home to her lonely place and poured herself a glass of Merlot and pulled out the manuscripts of the show from her bag. She had the first two episodes to proof, so she decided to work until she was ready to go to sleep. She put on her pajamas and wrapped her hair, sat in her favorite chair, and put her feet up on her ottoman. She had just grabbed her red Sharpie to get started when her doorbell rang. She looked at the clock and wondered who it could be. She tossed the script onto the ottoman and went for the door.

It was Jeff.

She paused, but opened the door. "Why are you here?"

"Can I come in?" he asked.

She folded her arms. "No, you can't, Jeff. Why are you here?"

"Listen, Tiff, I fucked up, okay? What I did was wrong and it is eating me up inside. I came by to ask you to forgive me and to give me another chance."

"Are you serious right now, Jeffrey? Two days ago, I come home and catch you in my bed with the hired help, and you thought I'd give you another chance? I forgive you and accept your apology, but another chance is not going to happen."

"Come on, Tiff, please. I am so sorry. I had a weak moment. She was here sashaying her ass around and in my face and I did a stupid thing. I was wrong. I am admitting that. I love you."

She wanted to laugh in his face. "Oh my God, Jeffrey. Listen, I have work to do and I don't have time for this. Good night!" she yelled.

She tried to close the door, but he stopped her. He grabbed her and kissed her deeply. She didn't stop him at first, but when he touched her breast, she pulled away.

"Jeff, you need to leave," she said and backed up.

"I need you, and I want another chance," he said.

Her eyes welled. "Jeff, the wound is still open, and I can't do this right now. I forgive you, okay, but that is all I can give you right now."

"Fair enough, Tiffany. You take all the time you need. Just know that I am sorry for what I did, and if you allow me another chance with you, I'll never hurt you again."

She wanted to believe him, but somehow she didn't. "Good night, Jeff." she said.

He walked away. She shut the door and contemplated whether she should open the door and let him in, but decided she wasn't going to let him come back so easy. She didn't want him to think for one second that what he did was okay.

Tiffany tried to get back to work, but now she couldn't focus. She cared for Jeff, yes, but she doubted she loved him. She was hurt by his actions, but for some reason, she wasn't hurt that the relationship ended. She wondered if she meant it when she said "I love you," or did she say it back because it was the thing to say when someone said it to you? Thinking about it, she realized she truly didn't mean it. At least she assumed she didn't, since she didn't feel like she was going to miss him much. Or maybe she already had high hopes for Kory and her judgment was being clouded.

She grabbed the script and managed to get back to work. She reread it a few times and when she looked up again, it was after midnight.

After taking her glass into the kitchen, she went back to her room and went to her closet to pick an outfit to wear to dinner the next night. She decided on a sleeveless, low-cut number that was made to undeniably get a man's attention. She hadn't worn it in months, so she removed it from the hanger to try it on.

"Perfect," she said, admiring her curves in the mirror. She stepped into her pumps and turned to the side, admiring her ass in her three-way mirror. It was plump and looked sensational, she thought and smiled. That would be her "first date with Kory" dress.

She took it off and hung it back up and headed to bed, but couldn't fall asleep. She lay awake imagining what the date would be like. Finally, she fell asleep, and before she knew it, her alarm was blaring.

Too tired to move, she called Myah and said she would be in later and then she went back to sleep for a couple more hours.

Chapter Five

Tiffany was dressed and ready to leave the house, but she couldn't relax. She felt like she did the night she lost her virginity to her boyfriend Shawn Knight, in her senior year of high school. The same butterflies she had then were flying around in her belly as she made her way to her car. When she walked into the restaurant, she felt sick. She rushed into the ladies' room and took a couple of deep, cleansing breaths. "Get it together, Tiffany," she told herself. "You are a grown-ass woman, and you should not be trembling." She took a couple more breaths before exiting the ladies' room. As soon as she opened the door, she spotted him. *He is looking damn good,* she thought as she moved toward him. When she got closer, she noticed a woman standing near him, and she almost fell on her face when she saw him put his hand on the small of her back. Just then, he saw Tiffany and waved her over.

"Tiffany," he called.

Caught off guard, she put on a smile. "Hi, ummm . . . Hi."

"Tiffany, how are you?" he asked. "This is my fiancée, Tressa. I hope you don't mind her joining us. When I told her that I ran into an old friend from high school who happens to be the producer for her favorite show, *Boy Crazy,* she begged to come along."

"Well, I didn't beg," the woman said. "Okay, I did, maybe a little." She extended her little, pretty hand. She was drop-dead gorgeous. There was not one imperfection about this woman that Tiffany could see. Even her hairline was flawless.

Code red. Code. Code red. Or blue. Hell, I don't know, whatever code they call when a person is dying, Tiffany thought as she shook Tressa's soft hand. *Rose.* She needed Rose to call at that particular moment and say there was an emergency. She couldn't stay because she was sure she'd pass out.

"No, of course I don't mind," she said. "Why would I mind a fan joining us for dinner? And you are getting married, that is great." She hoped it didn't sound as fake as it was.

"I knew you wouldn't," Kory said. "Are you ladies ready?" He held out his arms to escort both of them in.

They sat and Tiffany ordered a martini and asked for a shot of vodka. She felt herself shaking, and she kept blinking as she watched the love of her teenage life sit across from her with his beautiful fiancée.

They made small talk during their meals and Tiffany mostly poked at her food because she knew she'd vomit if she ate. Tressa was perfect, from her even white teeth to the deep dimples in her cheeks. *This was the longest dinner ever,* Tiffany thought, hoping the server would bring the check soon.

Tressa took a sip from her glass. "So, Tiffany, please tell me what's going to happen next season. I know it's going to be awesome."

"Tressa, you know I can't spill. That would go against my contract. But I will say that we are going to go out with a bang. KCLN is going to regret not renewing us after the next season." Tiffany waved for another drink. She knew she was overdoing it, but she wanted to relax. She was trying not to break out in tears.

"What? The other woman sounded shocked. "Get out. This is going to be *Boy Crazy*'s last season?"

"Sadly, yes," Tiffany said despondently. "Unless we can get another network to take us." The waiter came back with another apple martini and she grabbed it as soon as he placed it on the table.

"Well, why don't you come to us?" Tressa said.

"Us who?"

"TiMax," she said as if Tiffany should have known.

"Come again?" Tiffany said. Now she was interested in what the young beauty had to say. TiMax was a premium channel: a network on cable and dish where they said dirty words and had sex scenes.

Tressa slapped Kory's arm. "You didn't tell her, Kory?"

"Tell me what?"

"Langley Green is my father. He is one of the network's owners," Tressa proudly announced.

"Shut up!" Tiffany yelled in disbelief.

"No, he is."

"Shut up!" Tiffany said again in a higher pitch.

"Yes, and I can set you up to meet with him. And once I tell him that *Boy Crazy* is my favorite show and maybe whine a little, okay a lot," she said (Tiffany quickly realized that was her thing, her way of expression), "I'm sure my favorite show will have a slot, and boom, everybody wins."

Tiffany no longer felt sick to her stomach. "You'd do that for me?"

"Of course. You are my fiancé's old best bud."

Tiffany nodded, although she and Kory were never best buds. He didn't know about the hearts she drew around their names on all of her notebooks or the fact she would name her sons Kory One, Kory Two, Kory Three, and Kory Four. George Foreman did it, so why couldn't she?

"Tressa, that would be great. I don't know what to say. Thank you, I mean, wow." Tiffany was overjoyed. She couldn't wait to tell her team. This could be *Boy Crazy*'s big break. More money and more creative freedom.

"No, it would be my pleasure. Just give me a card and I'll have someone get in touch with you soon." Tiffany handed Tressa a card so fast she almost knocked over her drink. "Now, I need to run to the ladies' room," Tressa said and stood. She smiled and walked toward the rear of the restaurant.

"Kory, wow, I had no idea that you were engaged. That is awesome, and I am just, like, blown away right now trying to take it all in."

"Thank you, and I am still trying to take it all in myself. Tressa and I haven't been together too long, but she is amazing. A little whining, okay a lot of whining," he said imitating his fiancée. "Before I knew it, we were at the store picking out an engagement ring."

"Well, if you're marrying her, she must be special."

"Yes, she is. Spoiled, but special. My family has money too, but we grew up working hard. Reesy, Tressa, hasn't worked for anything."

"Well, I'm with you on that. My family didn't have money. My mom struggled with me and my brother, and when my brother was killed, my mom had a depressed moment and I became the woman of the house. I had to take care of her and me, so it was difficult."

"I remember that. I'm sorry; I forgot your brother was killed."

"It's okay," Tiffany said and gave a faint smile.

"Listen, we are having a cookout on Saturday. You should come and bring your boyfriend."

"What makes you think I have a boyfriend?"

"Come on, Tiff, you gotta be dating somebody. Look at you; you are smart and gorgeous as ever. I knew you'd blossom into a gorgeous woman."

She couldn't tell if he was sincere or being polite. "Come on. Kory, you barely noticed me in school."

"I noticed you; you just didn't know that I noticed."

Tressa returned to the table. "So, do we need another round or should we call it a night?" she asked.

"I think we should call it a night," Tiffany said. She tried to keep her eyes on Tressa to keep from looking Kory in the eyes. At that very moment, she wished Tressa would have never gone to the ladies' room and left her alone with him. His words were so smooth and tender. She wondered if he meant them or if he was just trying to make her feel good.

When she got into her car, she immediately dialed Rose. "What's up, diva? How was your date with your first love?" Rose asked.

"You mean with my first love and his fiancée? It was fabulous," Tiffany said with sarcasm.

"Hold the damn phone. Did you say fiancée?"

"Yes, his drop-dead gorgeous, perfect size-four fiancée. She looks like she just stepped out of *Essence* magazine. She isn't *Jet*'s beauty of the week beautiful, no. No, she is Nia Long, Paula Patten, slap yo' momma beautiful. Her skin, flawless. Her legs, silky. Her ass, plump. Her waist, tiny. And her breasts, oh my Lord, Rosie, only surgery could get my breasts to look that beautiful. I felt like an idiot." Tiffany took a breath. "Here I am, primping in the mirror, thinking I looked like Janet Jackson. But standing next to her, I look like Freddie Jackson."

Rose laughed.

"It's not funny, Rose," Tiffany moaned.

"Listen, Tiff, it couldn't have gone that bad. And you know skinny don't make you pretty," she reminded her. That's what they always said to cover their spite for the slimmer girls.

"I know, Rose, but she is truly gorgeous. I just wish he had told me he was engaged. I would have never asked him to dinner if I knew he was engaged."

"Awww, Tiff, I'm sorry it didn't go well," Rose said.

"Well, actually it did. Turns out that she is the daughter of Langley Green."

"Who is Langley Green?"

"One of the owners of TiMax. She is going to hook me up with a meeting with him to save my show."

"Get out. Tiffany, that is wonderful. See, it was meant for you to go on that dinner date."

"Yes, the Lord does work in mysterious ways. Oh, well, I guess I need to stop dreaming about Kory. He is not available." She sighed. "My love life sucks."

"Girl, join the club. Whose doesn't?"

"Tressa and Kory's," Tiffany said.

Rose laughed again. "Girl, you are silly."

"Oh, and let me tell you this. Tressa goes to the bathroom and Kory tells me that he noticed me back when we were in high school."

"Noticed you when?"

"That's what I'm saying. He gon' say he knew I'd blossom into a gorgeous woman. I was like, 'When did you notice me in high school,' and he was like, 'You didn't know that I did, but I did,' and threw me way off, because I don't know what the hell that was supposed to mean."

"Maybe he did, Tiff," Rose said.

"Yeah, maybe, but it doesn't matter now."

"Well, just focus on your show for now and let love happen when it happens."

"You're right, girl. Let me go so I can call Asia and fill her in and ask her to go to this barbeque with me on Saturday."

"What barbeque?"

"Kory invited me to a barbeque. I guess he will call me with the details because when Tressa came back to the table, he didn't mention it again."

"Damn, I wish I lived in L.A. It's getting cold here and there ain't no barbeques going on here," Rose said sadly.

"Tell me about it. I do not miss Old Man Winter," Tiffany said, and they laughed.

"Well, let me know how it goes with the meeting, and again, I'm sorry you lost Kory again."

"Yeah, me too. Love ya, girl."

"Love you too," Rose said and they hung up.

Pulling into her driveway at home, Tiffany dialed Asia.

Chapter Six

When Asia blew the horn, Tiffany came out. "Look at you, momma," Asia called, smiling at her friend. "Showing off those pretty legs of yours."

Tiffany had on a yellow halter and blue cutoff shorts. She had her hair up in a ponytail with a long extension added and her makeup was beautiful. She'd had one of the stylists from the show come over that afternoon to glam her up because she didn't want to be in the same room with Tressa without looking her best. "Thank you, Asia. I wanted to feel a little sexy today."

"Well, I don't know how you feel, but you look sexy as hell."

They headed over to Kory's. When they arrived, Asia was impressed to see valet. "Wow, Tiff, you didn't tell me it would be one of your celeb friends."

"I didn't know it would be this upscale either, Asia," Tiffany said. "Kory has money, yes, but

I thought it would be a little outdoor family event, not all this." They went inside. There were people everywhere.

"Tiff, you made it," Kory said when he spotted her.

"Hey, Kory." He gave her a quick peck and a brief hug. She turned to introduce him to Asia. "This is my girl, Asia. Asia, this is Kory."

"Nice to meet you," Asia said.

"You too," he said, shaking her hand. "Listen, don't get lost, I have some people I wanna introduce you to. And my cousin, Keith, is dying to see you."

"Keith lives here too? Why didn't you tell me?"

"'Cause we honestly hadn't had a chance to talk. Head out back, grab a couple drinks, and I'll be out in a sec," he said, and he was off.

They made their way to the back and Tiffany actually ran into some people she knew. Tressa came over while she was mingling. "Tiffany, you made it. It's so good to see you."

"Hey, Tressa, good to see you too. This is my girl, Asia. Asia, this is Kory's fiancée, Tressa." Asia and Tressa shook hands.

"Well," Tressa said, "you ladies make yourselves at home. I have people to greet." Giving them a smile, she left.

"Wow, she is flawless," Asia said.

"Told ya," Tiffany said and took a sip of her drink.

"There you are," Kory said.

When Tiffany turned around, she saw he was with Keith. "Keith, hey, how are you?"

He picked her up off the ground with a big hug. "I'm fine. Look at you . . . Tiffany Richardson. Girl, look at you," he said, giving her a spin. "Kory was right, you are gorgeous, girl." He gave her another hug.

"I told you," Kory said.

Tiffany blushed. "Oh my God, this is like crazy. To run into you guys in L.A."

"Well, I came out here first, and then Kory came and was back and forth for a minute, but business is booming out here. Celebrities are mostly our clientele out here, so the money is unquestionably better. We've been trying to convince Kennedy to come out here, but that girl is never gonna leave her daddy or Cher's side."

"Oh my God, Kennedy and Cher are still tight like that? They've been friends for like a million years."

"Cherae, yes, somehow they are still friends 'til this day. Kennedy and Cher are like two peas in a pod. You know Kory dated her for a minute."

"Man, shut up, that was a brief minute," Kory said. They laughed.

"You dated Cherae Thompson?"

"Yes, I did, now can we please change the subject." Tressa called for him. "I'll be back," he said and hurried over to see what she needed.

"So, where is this wife of yours, Keith?"

"She is on tour," he said.

"On tour? Who is your wife?"

"Janice Valentine. She is one of the members of Victory. You know the gospel group."

"No way. You married one of the sisters of Juliana Valentine? I know there was a huge scandal over her murder. I followed that story on the news. I'd love to meet her twin, Julia. I mean that story was huge. Wow, you married one of them?"

"Yes, as a matter of fact, Julia will be here soon."

"Julia Valentine is coming here today? She is like the biggest R&B artist on the planet. She is huge."

"Yes."

"Wow, I wonder if she could sing our new theme song. Better than that, come on to my show and sing on an episode. That would be epic. Then my show may get its contract."

"Just ask her, I'm sure she will."

"What? Just ask her? You want me to just walk up to her and say, 'Hey, I'm Tiffany Richardson and I want you to sing on an episode of my television show, *Boy Crazy*'?"

"Yep. Lia is a sweetheart, and if you ask, she will do it. I will introduce you to her when they arrive."

"Keith, don't play. Are you serious? You think she will?"

"I know she will."

"Wow, Keith, this is like . . . Wow. Wait 'til my staff hears this."

They continued to catch up and Asia excused herself.

"So, what's up with your love life, Miss Tiffany? Who is the lucky man in your life?"

"Ha," she said laughing. "There is no lucky man in my life. I had a man, but that went to shit."

"What? What? What happened?"

"Well, short version, I came home a little early after hearing that my show is in its final season and found him in my bed with my cleaning lady."

"What? No shit?"

"No shit. Then he showed up two days later apologizing and asking me for another chance. It was comical; it *is* comical, now that I think about it."

"Damn, sorry," Keith said sympathetically.

"It's cool. You win some, you lose some, they say." She took a swallow of her drink.

"You know Kory had a thing for you back in the day?"

"What? G'on wit' dat, Keith."

"He did," he said.

"Why am I hearing about this now, over fifteen years later?"

"Because back then, he thought a smart girl like you wouldn't be interested. Remember when y'all had chemistry together because he failed biology his freshman year and he needed that science credit to graduate?"

"Yeah, I remember that," she said, thinking back.

"Y'all worked on a project together."

"Yes, and the day before it was due, he come telling me that he didn't finish his part, meaning he didn't do it at all. I stayed up all night doing what he had two weeks to do, just so he wouldn't bring down my grade."

"Yes, and that A you made on that project helped him to pass with a D. If it weren't for you, he would not have graduated that June. He talked about you for the rest of that summer."

"No way," she said, shocked.

"Yes," he said.

She looked over at Kory. He caught her eye and he smiled. She smiled back, and then Tressa walked over and put her arms around his neck and kissed him. Tiffany's smile faded.

She and Keith got up and mingled. When Julia finally made it, Keith introduced her to Tiffany, and it was as painless as asking and the singer agreed to be a guest on an episode. She gave Tiffany her cell number and told her to let her know when. She couldn't wait to tell her staff she got Julia Valentine to appear on a show.

"Hey, Tiffany," Kory said. A man accompanied him. "I want you to meet Vi. He is a song writer at Universal Records. If you want a new theme song for your show when you get your new contract with TiMax, he is your man. And he from the Chi."

"Southside, baby," Vi said and gave her a quick friendly hug and kiss.

"Nice to meet you, Vi, and I definitely need your number, because when this new contract comes through, we gon' need a hot new theme song." Tiffany was excited. She started to feel like things were going to work out just fine.

"No doubt. Now let me see you and Kory on this bid whist table. You can play right?"

"Fo'sho," she said and followed them.

"Yo, Keith, we found a player. These L.A. fools don't know nothing about bid," Vi yelled.

They were set to play. Kory gave Tiffany a high five. They were partners against Vi and Keith. Tressa hung on Kory's neck like a necklace the entire game, and when Tiffany and Kory beat them, she frowned at their victory celebration. Tiffany noticed the look on Tressa's face and decided to cut it short.

"I am going to get me another drink," she said and headed toward the bar.

"And hurry back, so we can show these L.A. peeps how to step," Vi yelled after her.

When Tiffany rejoined them, they all went out to the dance floor that had been laid over the grass under a gigantic tent. Stepping onto the floor with Vi, Tiffany heard Kory ask Tressa to dance. She started to dance, but watched them from the corner of her eye, still listening. Though the music was loud, the couple spoke loud enough that she was able to hear them.

"Come on, come dance with me," he asked.

"No, Kory," Tressa said, "you know I don't know how to step. I'm not gon' go out there and make a fool out of myself."

"Come on, baby, I will show you."

"No, I'm gonna look foolish trying to do that stupid step mess."

"It's not stupid, Reesy," he said pulling her close. "Come on, dance with yo' man."

When she refused again, he shrugged and stepped onto the dance floor without her. He cut in and took Tiffany's hand out of Vi's. Vi didn't argue.

Tiffany had a ball. As the night came to an end, the crowd got lighter. When she was ready to go, she left the dance floor and found Asia. Asia had met someone, however, and wasn't ready to go, so Tiffany went out front and took a seat on one of the little benches. Shortly after, Kory walked out and found her there.

"Hey, there you are," he said. She looked up. "I thought you left without saying good-bye."

"No, I was ready to leave, but my ride is not ready," she said.

"Well, I can give you a ride," he offered.

"Naw, that may not be a good idea. Your fiancée may not approve."

"Tressa isn't like that."

Just then, Tressa walked out. From the look on her face, Tiffany could tell she wasn't happy to find him alone with her. "Sweetie, I need you real quick," she said.

Tiffany smiled as Kory got up and went inside with her.

Keith ended up giving her a ride home.

Chapter Seven

"So what's the deal with you and your home-girl?" Tressa asked when Kory stepped out of the shower.

"What do you mean, Reesy?"

"Exactly what I said, Kory. Did you ever date her?"

"No, we were just cool in school. She used to hang out with my li'l cousin, Kennedy. We had a couple classes together back in school. I used to see her around. It is just good to catch up with her."

"Well, did she like you?"

"Hey, I know the queen of L.A. is not jealous of my old high school homegirl?" he asked. He embraced her from behind and planted soft kisses on her neck.

"No. Hell no, I'm not jealous. I just don't enjoy seeing my man have a grand old time with another woman."

"Reesy, you are my center, okay? It's fun to hang out with folks that know how to step or play bid and can share stories of food from home. We just had fun catching up. Tiffany is harmless." He turned her to face him.

She gazed into his hazel eyes and believed him. No way was that "big-boned" heifer going to take her man. "I'm not jealous and I'm not tripping," she said.

"Good, and one more thing and I'll drop the Tiffany subject."

"What's that?"

"Can you please remember to holla at your dad about her show? She really needs a break, babe. Last night, I watched a couple episodes on Netflix, and you were right, it is a great show."

"Okay, I will holla at Daddy, but I can't make any promises."

"I know, babe, but I know your father won't tell you no. Her show is really good, and I know he will sign them if you ask." He kissed her deeply and let his towel drop to the floor. She could feel his massive erection. "Suck it for me, baby," he whispered.

She hated when he asked her for head. She kissed his chest down to his stomach then went down in a squat to take him inside of her mouth. She licked the head a little bit, and he closed his eyes and tilted his head back. When she put it in her mouth and began to go up and down on it, his eyes popped open and he pulled back.

"Careful, Reesy, your teeth," he said. She slowed down, pulled back, and teased his head with her tongue again. When she began sucking him again, he pulled back again.

"Reesy, baby, your teeth."

"I'm sorry, your dick is just so big."

He pulled her up. "Don't worry about it. You don't have to do that. Just let me slide it in." He lifted her up onto the vanity.

"Condom, Kory," she instructed.

"Reesy, why are you on the pill if I still have to use rubbers?"

"Because I told you, I'm not taking any chances. You will get it without the plastic when we are married."

He went for a Magnum and when he got back to her, she saw that his dick had gone down. "You wanna help me get it back up?" he asked.

She frowned. "How?"

"By touching me." He took her hand and put it on him for her to stroke him.

Sighing inwardly, she stroked his shaft with no enthusiasm. He lifted her nightgown and went to suck on her nipple. She looked up at the ceiling. She knew there were thirty-eight and a half tiles.

"Awww, Kory, not so hard," she complained. He loosened his suction and moved to the other nipple.

Noticing his mouth was no longer on her breast, she looked at him and found him staring at her.

"Do you wanna do this, Reesy?"

"Not really." she said.

He stopped and backed away. "What's wrong, Reesy Cup? Since I slid that ring on your finger two weeks ago, you've become uninterested in making love to me. What's wrong?"

"Nothing, Kory," she said, pulling down her gown. "It seems that is all you wanna do." She slid off the vanity.

"Reesy, you haven't had sex with me since the night we got engaged. That was two weeks ago. All I've been getting from you since that night are excuses. 'Baby, I'm tired' or 'My head hurts' or 'I can't come over tonight, daddy.'"

"Damn, Kory, don't start," she yelled. "I'm not a sex object. You think because we are engaged that I'm supposed to just fuck you whenever your dick is hard."

"Reesy, you know that's not true. I waited eight weeks to get it from you. Two whole months. We've been together for six months, and in the last two weeks, no ass. I know you are not a sex object, but you are my woman. I love you, Reesy, and I want to make love to you. How is that treating you like a sex object?" She looked at him, but didn't answer. "I'm going for a run," he said, going to his dresser.

"A run, Kory, seriously?" She sneered. "Or are you going to call your girl, Tiffany, to please your dick?"

"Yes, a run, Reesy. And Tiffany and I aren't fucking around. If we were, I wouldn't be here begging you for ass. I'd be with her instead of your ass," he snapped.

Tressa hadn't expected him to come back hard at her. Normally, she'd have him apologizing to her even if she was the one who was wrong.

"Look, sweetheart," she said, softening her tone. "I'm sorry, okay? I don't want to fight. And if you want to make love, we can make love. I just had a long day and the party drained me, but it has absolutely nothing to do with you. I want to make love to you, Kory. I'm sorry for yelling."

She walked over and caressed him from behind, planting soft kisses on his back. Her soft touch made his manhood rise again and she felt the tension leave his body. He turned to her and she lifted her gown over her head.

He kissed her and caressed her face. "I love you, Reesy, and you ought to know that I would never treat you like an object or cheat on you. I only want to be with you."

"I know," she said. She pulled him toward the bed, climbed in, and lay on her back. He pushed his boxer briefs down and moved to climb on top of her. "Kory, condom, please," she whispered.

He got another one and rolled it on, then came down on her and began to kiss her as he slid inside her body. He moved slow and she knew he was trying to prolong it. She worked her body back on his to help get it over with. When he collapsed on her, his face buried in her neck, she grimaced. He got up to flush the condom and she quickly got underneath the covers. He came back into the room, turned out the light, and got in bed, scooting close to her.

"No round two?" he whispered.

"Baby, I'm exhausted," she said.

Kory kissed the side of her head. "Okay," he said.

"Can you back up a bit, it's hot," she complained. In the darkness, she felt him shake his head, but he rolled over to his side of the bed.

"Good night," he said, sounding irritated.

"Good night, and, don't forget we have a ten o'clock with Amber to go over the details for the engagement party."

"I won't," he said.

***

"Which one do you like?" Tressa asked.

Kory honestly didn't care. He'd lain awake the previous night wanting to tell her to go home and wondering if he should have ever proposed. "Reesy, it doesn't matter, baby, they are both nice." He was ready for the meeting to be over already.

"The white ones," she told Amber. Her best friend was also her event planner.

"And do you guys have your guest list yet?" Amber asked.

"No, we are still working on it," Tressa answered.

"Well, I need it no later than Tuesday."

"We'll have it, no worries," Tressa told her. Kory wondered why she had even invited him. Earlier in the meeting, everything she asked him, she chose the opposite of what he suggested. After the fourth time that happened, he was ready to get up and walk out. Instead, he shut down and started texting Keith. He'd do an occasional nod, but he wasn't paying attention to details.

"Kory, why don't you get the car and I'll be out in a sec," Tressa said. He didn't mind one bit.

As soon as Kory was out of earshot, Tressa turned back to her friend. "So what should I do about this Tiffany situation?"

Amber was busy putting her samples into her designer valise. "Reesy, I didn't know there was a 'Tiffany situation.' She talked more to Keith than with Kory."

"Ummm, hello, Amber, you were at the party last night. You saw how they carried on. And then he asked me again to talk to my father about her stupid show."

"Well, why did you open your big mouth in the first place if you didn't have any intentions on helping her?"

"Because I was trying to impress Kory. When he told me he was meeting an old friend from home for dinner, you know I was suspicious. I couldn't let my man go to dinner alone without checking this bitch out, so I pretended to love *Boy Crazy* so he would take me with. Then I see this high-yellow, cornbread-fed bombshell walk out with all these curves in the sexiest dress she owns. And that shit made me wonder if she was just an old friend or an ex-girlfriend.

"I saw the look on her face when she saw me. She thought her and Kory were meeting alone. As cool as she tried to play it, she gave herself away by ordering an apple martini with a shot of vodka to start. That was a sure sign of nervousness. She had no idea Kory was engaged, I could see it on her face. I had to say something to show Kory how jealous I wasn't and win some points."

"But, Reesy, you are jealous, and you have no reason to be. Kory loves you. You made that brother wait two months for some ass, and he stuck around. After you finally gave him some, you slapped him with the 'I love you' and somehow convinced him to propose to you within six months, even though you purposely scrape his dick with your teeth to get out of giving him blow jobs. If that's not love, I don't know what is."

"I know Kory loves me, Amber, and sex is just overrated. I'd rather wear last season's clothing out in public than have a man all on top of me. And you know I detest oral sex. It is repulsive. If I keep doing a horrible job, he won't ask."

"But you love for him to do you?"

"Yes. And if that's all he did and then let me go to sleep, life would be perfect."

Amber shook her head. "You have issues, Reesy. I'm telling you now Kory is one of the good ones. He is not like the athletes, actors, or rappers you've dated in the past who have broken your heart over and over again. He has wealth because he is a smart businessman, not because he compromises his values for a buck. Don't turn this into a Tressa sitcom. Relax and trust him. You are Tressa Isabella Green. Kory accepts you for who you are, even though you have a tabloid past; that means something. Don't lose another one, Reesy. Be happy for once and ditch the drama." She stood up.

"So you think I have nothing to worry about?" Reesy asked.

"Nothing. And call your dad and put a good word in for that sister like you said you would. Smooches." She gave Tressa a quick peck and a hug. "And I need that list by Tuesday, Reesy," she reminded her as she walked away. "I'm serious."

"You'll have it!" Tressa called after her. She sat back down. She didn't care what Amber said. She wasn't new to the game; she knew Tiffany had an agenda. She pulled out her phone to call her dad, but then put it back in her purse. She wasn't going to ask her father to help her potential competition. She got up, grabbed her expensive bag and sunglasses, and went out to the car where she knew Kory was waiting patiently. When he saw her approaching, he got out and opened her door.

"So, babe," she said when he got back in, "you think we can swing by Saks? I got a call that my shoes are in." She locked her seatbelt and he started the car.

"Babe, I told you that I have to meet up with the fellas. We are going to the game."

his phone back on his nightstand
into bed. They got up later and he
head to the jewelry store, while she
head to TiMax.

on't forget to holla at your dad about
show," he reminded her again. "She
eds this break."

't, for the last time. I will see you later,"
d and kissed him bye.

en she arrived to her dad's office, she
ed with him for a bit, but never said a word
ut Tiffany's show. Leaving his office, she ran
o Wallace. He was one of the producers there
d he was madly in love with her. She had a
rilliant idea.

"Wallace, how are you?" This was the first time
she addressed him before he spoke to her. She
usually avoided him at all cost because he was
an annoying-ass groupie.

"I'm great, Miss Green," he said with a bright
smile. "How are you?" He was a geek, but he
was good-looking. The package he was in was all
wrong. *A good-looking square. What a waste of
fine,* she thought because he was a joke.

"I'm good. And you are looking good today.
Is that a new shirt?" He looked surprised and
she knew he was shocked she'd said that many
words to him.

"That's today?" she asked, surprised.

"Yes, Reesy. I just reminded you this morning,"
he said as he pulled out the club's drive.

"This will only take a sec, babe. And we're
already on this side of town."

"Reesy, I am already thirty minutes behind."

"Kory, it's like five minutes away. If you are
already behind, what difference will five minutes
make?"

Not wanting to continue to go back and forth,
he agreed to go. Kory pulled up in front of Saks
and Tressa hopped out. He knew her 'I'll be
right back' meant he was going to be even later
meeting the guys. He banged his head back
against the headrest. How did he let her do
this to him all the time? His phone rang and
his frown turned upside down when he saw
Tiffany's name.

"Hey," he said when he answered.

"Hey, this is Tiff," she said. He heard the smile
in her voice.

"I know, what's up, girl?"

"Nothing too much. Keith told me that you
guys had plans to go to the game today, so I
wanted to catch you before it started to say
thanks for having me and Asia over yesterday. I
had a ball. I hadn't danced like that in ages."

"Sure, of course. I am so happy you came. Vi

texted me this morning asking for a rematch since we whipped their asses so bad last night in bid."

"Yes, we tore them a new one," she said.

"We are going to have to get together and do it again soon."

"Yes, indeed." They lapsed into a weird silence until she spoke again. "Well, I don't want to keep you. I just wanted to thank you and Tressa for having us."

At the mention of his fiancée's name, he blinked. The pleasant sound of Tiffany's tone had given him a brief moment of amnesia. Reesy tapped on the glass and he ended the call and hit the lock.

"Who was that?"

"Keith," he lied. He didn't want to get anything started with Tressa. He just wanted to drop her and get to Keith's so they could head to the game.

"Oh, okay," she said.

She placed
and got back
got ready to
dressed to
"Babe, d
Tiffany's
really ne
"I wo
she sa
Wh
chat
abo
int
a
b

Chap

Tressa was up before Ko
She got up, and went over
bed, and eased his cell phone
stand and went into the bathr
his call history and texts. She w
logs and there it was. An incoming
Tiffany at 1:06 p.m. from the day befor
known he'd been lying when she got ba
the car. She went to his texts and was relie
to see that there were only four messages. On
from Tiffany asking how was the game, Kory
replying that it was great, her saying okay
good night, and him saying it back. That was
harmless, but she didn't want them to be
talking and texting on a regular. She went to
his contacts and was about to delete Tiffany's
number, but decided she'd better not. If she
did, he'd know she'd been in his phone. She
wanted to keep that on the low so she could
check it again at a later date.

"This old thing? I've worn it a million times."
She knew he was telling the truth, because it
looked as if he had worn it two million times.

"Well, that color is working on you," she lied.
"Listen, can I talk to you in your office for a
minute?"

"Sure," he said, giving her a nervous smile.

"Listen," she said once he closed the door. "I
have this dilemma and I was wondering if you
could help me out." She knew he would be eager
to help her.

"Anything for you," he said.

"I have this friend who is trying to bring her
show over to TiMax, but I don't think it would
be a great fit. Being the sweetheart that I am, I
sorta promised her I'd set something up with
my dad to share her proposal. But you know, I
don't want to bother Daddy with this. I was only
being polite, but now she is hounding me, and I
need someone to let her down gently. So, I was
wondering if you'd see her, hear her out, and tell
her you will get back to her after you present this
to my dad. Then, in a couple days, call her and
tell her that he declined."

"Wow, who is she?"

"Tiffany Richardson."

"At KCLN?"

Tressa frowned. "Yeah, do you know her?"

"No, but I've heard great things. She took her show from number six to number one in one season. *Boy Crazy* is hot and could be a good fit for TiMax. Is KCLN not going to renew her contract?"

"Wallace, I'm not sure. The thing is, TiMax cannot take her show."

"Why?"

"Okay, Wallace, I'll be straight with you. She is my fiancé's ex-girlfriend from Chicago. Until Kory and I are married, we don't need any distractions."

"Okay, Miss Green, enough said. When do you want me to meet her?"

"Whenever you want. Here is her number." She slid Tiffany's card across his desk and he picked it up. "Just decline her before my engagement party," she instructed.

"Done," he said.

She stood up and walked over to the other side of his desk and got into his face like she was going to kiss him. "If you pull this off, I will make sure you have a long career here at TiMax."

"No worries, I got this," he said.

"I'm sure you do, daddy," she said, flirting a little. She knew his nerdy ass got a hard on. She gave him a little wink and reminded him that this needed to stay between them and he winked back.

She wanted to laugh in his dumb-ass face, but she held on to her laughter until she made it down the hall. She left and hit a few stores and went by to visit her mom before she headed to Kory's. When she walked in, the aroma of food hit her nose and she knew he was cooking.

"Sweetheart?" she yelled and stepped out of her shoes.

"In here," he yelled from the kitchen.

When she walked in, he had on a tank, some basketball shorts, socks and slippers, and his KISS THE COOK apron. Kory was a little over six feet, medium brown, and had a strong jaw line that made his tapered beard look like layers of chocolate waves. He had a nice grade of hair, but wore it low, and his line was never over-grown. He had hazel eyes that she had learned he got from his mother, and his lashes were so long they looked like girl lashes. He was fine and smart and had a cockiness about himself that she admired.

"Hey," she said and went over to kiss him.

"Hey, baby, how was your day?"

"It was great. I got some shopping done, went by the network, and stopped by to visit my mom."

"Speaking of the network, thanks so much for hollering at your dad for Tiff. She got a call today already from that cat, Wallace Mitchell, and she was like on ten."

"Sure. I told you I would." She grabbed the red wine from the fridge and poured herself a glass. "Now that she has the interview, maybe she'll quit blowing up your phone." She took a seat at the island.

"Tiffany has not been blowing up my phone," Kory protested.

"Whatever." She took a sip of wine.

"Okay, Reesy, if you say so."

She watched him put the foil back over the salmon and put it back into the oven. "Oh, and after dinner, we have to do this invite list."

"Listen, Reesy, you handle that. Most of my people are in Chicago. My parents, uncles, and my cousin Kennedy are coming into town next Thursday. There will be less than twenty-five people on my list."

"So write them down," she snapped and shot him a look.

"Grab that pad from the fridge," he instructed.

"Okay," she said and when she did, he gave her his quick list. "Oh, and Tiffany plus one," he added.

known that. "What?" she aske
ry knew.

u only been here, what, a minu
ve time, I got the inside track

decided to get back to the meeti
ow on to my good news."
s more?" Myah asked.

ver the weekend, I got to meet the gr
alentine and she has agreed to appear
ow and sing a song," she announced a
went nuts. Julia Valentine was bigger th
twin sister was when she was alive.

hut the front door," Darryl said.

Tiffany wondered how he could be gay on th
vel. He bypassed Sugarland a thousand tim
n the gay scale. "I'm not lying. She even ga
me her cell number. She's the sister-in-law
an old friend. He is married to her sister, Jani
Valentine, from the gospel group Victory."

"Oh, there is a God," Myah shouted.

"Listen up, everyone, seriously. We need to p
everything we have into this last season. I mea
we have to sit in this room and write 'til o
hands bleed." She turned to the three main ca
members. "And you ladies have to come wit
it this season. I am going to need you to give
more than your best. Moving over to a premiu

She rolled her eyes. "I hope she brings a date and not her girlfriend." She made air quotes when she said the last word.

"You will never quit, will you?" Kory poured rice into a serving dish from the pot.

"What?"

"First she wants me, and now she's a lesbian? Come on, Reesy, babe, cut it out. If you would get to know her, you just might like her."

She laughed.

"What's funny?" he asked, taking the fish out of the oven.

"I don't need to get to know her. I have enough friends. It doesn't matter if she is gay or straight; what matters is what she wants with you."

"Okay, cut." Kory put the pan down. "Let's clear this up right now. And after I say this, I would like for you to let this go. I want you and only you. I proposed to you. Tiffany is an old friend; that is it. Let's just say your theory is right, and she wants me. It doesn't matter, because I am with you."

"But—"

"No buts, Tressa. I love you." He walked around to the other side of the island and kissed her softly on the lips.

She smiled. "Okay, Kory, okay."

He kissed her again. "So no more 'terrible Tiffany' conversations."

"Okay," she agreed and tried to let it go. Maybe she was overthinking things. She was L.A.'s queen, so why was she so intimidated by Tiffany, who was a nobody? She felt better.

"Okay, now let's eat," Kory said.

Tiffany hadn't
wondering if K
"Yes, girl, yo
When you ha
that ho."
Tiffany
"Anyway,
"There
"Yes,
Julia V
the s
er

"Okay, everyone,
Feeling like she was abo
until everyone settled do
one of the most exciting days
good news and great news."

"Come on, already," Myah yelled.

"Okay, do you want the good news o
news?"

"Tiff, I'm dying here," Darryl yelled an
his eyes.

"I got a meeting with Wallace Mitche
TiMax on Thursday," she announced. Everyo
applauded.

"How did you get in the door?" Darryl asked.

"Well, an old friend from high school is engaged to Tressa Green, the daughter of a Mr. Langley Green and she hooked me up."

"Your old high school bud is engaged to the queen of L.A.? This is like her tenth fiancé," he said.

network means we can do whatever we want. No censorship, so you ladies are going to have to be prepared to step up your game and be ready to work. I mean, profanity, nudity; there are no limits with TiMax, and I want to make sure we are all on board."

Everyone nodded, some yelling, "Hell yeah."

"If we get this, we are going to reach a broader audience. It's game time people," she said. The meeting went on for another hour or so, and then she went into her office. Within a few minutes, Todd came in. She knew Brad had been the one to spill.

"Todd," she said nervously.

"Calm down, Tiff, I'm unarmed," he announced.

Her tension released. "I supposed you heard?"

"Yeah, white peeps do stick together," he joked with his hip-hop imitation.

"Are you pissed?"

"No, actually I'm proud. You stood your ground and I admire your drive."

"Thank you, Todd. You know this network left me no choice?"

"I know, and you will be missed. You came in here and did your thing, and I hope you have even more success with the new network."

"Thank you, Todd."

"You're welcome, just remember me if I end up on the unemployment line."

"No doubt. It was my luck walking in the wrong office, but you gave me my chance to shine and I won't forget it," she said and smiled.

"Okay, kid, keep doin' you," he said mocking her. Every time he asked her what was up, her reply was, "I'm doin' me."

Tiffany sat outside of Wallace's office and her knees wouldn't stop shaking. She was excited, but nervous. She had her pitch down and she felt great. When he finally called her in, she blew out a deep breath and sent up another silent prayer. The meeting lasted a couple hours and it went so well she wasn't worried. Afterward, she got in the car and called Kory. She wanted to tell Tressa thanks again.

"So it went well?" He sounded excited for her.

"Yes, and I'm feeling high right now. I wanted to tell Tressa thank you again."

"Well, I will tell her tonight when she calls. Her and her mom went to San Diego this morning to look at wedding gowns."

"That's cool. I just wanted to thank her. I mean, I'm so excited I'm about to burst."

"Where are you?"

d. "Oh my God, Kory, it was
in there, right? Nervous as hell,
s so nice. He let me tell him the
nted to go in for the new season
hat *Boy Crazy* would be the next
nce *Sex and the City*, only with black
e laughed. The bartender set her
ront of her and she took a sip. "I'm so
just know this is going to work out. I
it."

ow it will. Even though Reesy gets what-
she wants, I'm sure once you go in there
do you, they are going to be blown away," he
sincerely.

You really think so?" she asked, looking him
his eyes.

"Yes." He took a sip of his drink. "Confession . . ."

"What?" she asked curiously.

"I purchased the last three seasons on DVD
yesterday after Reesy left and I'm like three
episodes away from season three."

She was surprised. "You watched my show?"

"Yeah, I did, and to be honest, it's a good show.
Now, my parents would have beaten my ass for
some of the shit these girls do, but hey." They
laughed. "Like that episode when Joy took her
parents' BMW on a joyride and wrecked it. Now,
Kendal Banks would have torn me a new one."

"Heading ho...

"Why do...

Keith an...

"Gre...

"Of cou...

you the plac...

They hung u... not happy to hear... ran home and did a ... up her face. When she g... to say she was there. He te... at the bar. She spotted him a...

He immediately stood and hu... you look fantastic."

"Thank you, so do you." They sat dow... is Keith?"

"Well, he couldn't make it. His baby is ru... a fever, so . . ." He shrugged and took a sip of h... drink. "Where is Asia?"

"She had papers to grade and yada, yada, yada."

He signaled for the bartender. "Well, I guess it's just us. What would you like?" he asked when the bartender came over.

"Cosmo please," she said. The man nodded and went to make it right away.

"So tell me all the details about your meeting today," Kory said.

Tiffany grinne... awesome. I went... but Wallace wa... direction I wa... and he said ... best thing si... chicks." S... drink in f... excited. ... can feel... "I kn... ever ... and ... sai...

"Heading home."

"Why don't we meet for drinks? I can call Keith and we can go out and celebrate."

"Great, do you mind if Asia tags along?"

"Of course not, the more the merrier. I'll text you the place," he said.

They hung up and Tiffany called Asia. She was not happy to hear that she couldn't make it. She ran home and did a quick change and freshened up her face. When she got there, she texted Kory to say she was there. He texted back that he was at the bar. She spotted him and went over.

He immediately stood and hugged her. "Wow you look fantastic."

"Thank you, so do you." They sat down. "Where is Keith?"

"Well, he couldn't make it. His baby is running a fever, so . . ." He shrugged and took a sip of his drink. "Where is Asia?"

"She had papers to grade and yada, yada, yada."

He signaled for the bartender. "Well, I guess it's just us. What would you like?" he asked when the bartender came over.

"Cosmo please," she said. The man nodded and went to make it right away.

"So tell me all the details about your meeting today," Kory said.

Tiffany grinned. "Oh my God, Kory, it was awesome. I went in there, right? Nervous as hell, but Wallace was so nice. He let me tell him the direction I wanted to go in for the new season and he said that *Boy Crazy* would be the next best thing since *Sex and the City*, only with black chicks." She laughed. The bartender set her drink in front of her and she took a sip. "I'm so excited. I just know this is going to work out. I can feel it."

"I know it will. Even though Reesy gets whatever she wants, I'm sure once you go in there and do you, they are going to be blown away," he said sincerely.

"You really think so?" she asked, looking him in his eyes.

"Yes." He took a sip of his drink. "Confession . . ."

"What?" she asked curiously.

"I purchased the last three seasons on DVD yesterday after Reesy left and I'm like three episodes away from season three."

She was surprised. "You watched my show?"

"Yeah, I did, and to be honest, it's a good show. Now, my parents would have beaten my ass for some of the shit these girls do, but hey." They laughed. "Like that episode when Joy took her parents' BMW on a joyride and wrecked it. Now, Kendal Banks would have torn me a new one."

She laughed. "Or the episode when Claire's mom told her that she could not borrow her diamond studs and she dropped one down the drain. They tried to disconnect the pipe to get it out and flooded her mom's master bathroom. Now that idea came from me wearing a pair of hoops my mom said not to wear and I lost one in gym. Little did I know, they were real gold and my momma whipped my ass for that."

They laughed some more and reminisced on their childhood. Two hours and a few drinks later, they were good and tipsy.

"Okay, I think we should get a cab," he suggested.

"Yes, because I am in no condition to drive." She stood and had to grab hold of the barstool because she lost her balance. That made her laugh.

"Are you okay?"

"Describe okay," she said and they laughed.

"Okay, since I am less drunk than you, I will get you a cab and make sure you get home safe."

"No, I can't ask you to do that. I will be fine, Kory." She slurred a little. "You live on the hill where the rich citizens live. Our places are like forty-five minutes apart." She giggled.

In her state, he didn't trust putting her in a cab alone. "Come on, Tiff, let's go, sweetheart." He took her by the hand and grabbed her purse. She wasn't too drunk to walk, but she wasn't able to drive.

"Wait, wait, wait," she said.

He stopped. "What's wrong?"

"I really, really, really need to take off these shoes." She burst into laughter.

He laughed with her. "Okay, just step out of them and I will carry them."

"Thank you," she said and leaned against him to take them off.

With her purse and shoes in hand, he hailed a cab. When they got inside it, he asked for her address. She told the driver her street, but not her house number.

"Hold on," Kory said and went into her purse. He pulled out her license and gave the driver the address. She rested in his arms and dozed off. When they arrived, he woke her. "Tiff, wake up." He shook her.

"Huh?" Her head popped up.

"We are here," he said.

"Oh, Kory, thank you," she said taking her purse and shoes. She was a little more sober after her nap.

"No problem."

"You should come in," she suggested.

"Naw, I'm going to go home."

"Kory, that's nonsense. It's late. I'll put on a pot of coffee. In the morning, we can cab it back to our cars." He gave in and they went inside. She turned on the light. "Please make yourself at home. I am going to put on a pot and shower really quick, okay?"

He nodded and sat on the sofa. When he looked at his phone, he saw that he had five missed calls from Tressa.

"Where the hell have you been and why did you not answer my calls?" she asked when he called her back.

"Calm down, Reesy. I was out with Vi and we were having drinks. I just got in and saw I missed your calls."

"Don't lie to me."

"Reesy, where else would I be?"

"Kory, if you are lying to me, I swear this wedding is off!" she yelled.

"Reesy, I've had a few drinks, I'm tired, and I can't do this with you tonight. Either you trust me or you don't."

"Okay, I will see you tomorrow evening. We won't be back until close to dinner."

"Okay," he said.

"Okay, Kory, I love you," she said.

"I love you too," he said before hanging up.

A little later, Tiffany came out in cotton PJs and her face scrubbed clean. Kory sat up when she approached.

"How do you take your coffee?" she asked.

"One cream, two sugars," he said.

She went to pour both of them a cup. She handed him his and took a seat at the other end of the sofa.

"I'm sorry," she said.

"For what?"

"For drinking too much and making you lie to your fiancée."

He laughed a little. He hadn't known she'd heard him call Tressa. "You don't have to apologize, Tiff. I didn't lie for me. I lied for you," he said.

"What do you mean?"

"I have no problems with telling Reesy the truth. I can handle her and my relationship. I just know how important your career and your show is to you, and I don't want to do anything to hinder that. You are talented and you are passionate about what you are doing, and I do hope Mr. Green contracts your show. It will be a hit."

She smiled and he smiled back at her. Her smile was beautiful. He saw the teenager he had a thing for back in the day and he had to admit that there was more to it than there should have been.

"Thank you, Kory. And thank you for thinking of my career. I would never want to put you in a situation where you have to lie to her about hanging out with me, so after tonight, maybe we shouldn't hang anymore. I mean, I can understand why Tressa feels the way she feels, because if we were engaged, I wouldn't want you hanging with her."

"No, we can't stop being friends, Tiff. Now that you are back in my life, I don't want to not ever see you again."

"Huh?" she asked.

"I just don't think that us not being friends is the right answer, that's all," he said, realizing he should not have said "back in his life."

"I don't want to cause problems for you, Kory."

He put his coffee down and moved to her end. "You won't," he said. He hated that he wanted to kiss her. He looked at her beautiful face and caressed her cheek. "Listen, Tiff, it's been great seeing you again and hanging out with you. I just don't want to never see you again."

"Okay," she said and looked down. "Listen, I'm gonna turn in." She stood up. "Let me show you to the guest room." She led him to his room and turned on the light. "The fridge is full and you are welcome to make yourself at home."

"Okay. Thanks, Tiffany," he said.

Tiffany went to her room. She lay there and stared at the ceiling, telling herself not to get up and go back into the guest room. She wanted to lie next to Kory. She wanted him to hold her, but she knew it wouldn't be right. Finally she fell asleep, and the next day she woke up after ten.

She was late for work, but she didn't care. She headed straight to her guest room to wake him, but the bed was empty. She went into the front to look for him and found a note on her chalkboard saying, HAVE A GOOD DAY! He had drawn a smiley face.

She smiled and went back to her room to get ready for work.

Chapter Ten

Tiffany sat at her desk tapping her pen. It had been three days since her meeting with Wallace and since she'd last seen or heard from Kory. She was on edge and thought she would lose it. She stared at Wallace's card for hours, fighting the urge to call him. She wanted so badly to hear the verdict. She didn't want to go into the idea room without news, but what could she do, she didn't have any news. She grabbed her notes and went in. Everyone seemed to feel like she did and she understood.

"Okay, people," she said, "we have six more episodes to write. I need to know what episode you are on and where we are. We have less than a month before we start taping, so give it to me."

They all opened their notebooks. Darryl started reading and they read through the script for episode eighteen. It was good, Tiffany had to admit, but her mind was on TiMax.

"Okay, that was great, you guys. We are going to have a slamming season," she said.

"Then what?" Darryl asked.

"I don't know, Dee. It is on my mind every second too, you guys, but we gotta have faith. This is gonna work, so please, enough with the sad faces. As a matter of fact, go to your offices, grab your purses and wallets, and let's take a long lunch."

They went out as a group and ate and drank. When they came back, they were all smiles until they hit their floor. Myah was standing by the reception desk and she looked as if her mother died. All the laughter ceased.

"Mee-Mee, what?" Tiffany asked. "What is it?"

Myah's eyes welled. "Wallace Mitchell called while you guys were out and TiMax declined the show."

Tiffany grabbed her chest. She thought she'd have a heart attack right then and there. "Excuse me," she said and ran to the stairwell.

They were twenty-five stories up, but she ran all the way down the stairs. By the time she got to the bottom, she was crying uncontrollably. She dug around her purse for her phone and when she retrieved it, she called Kory first, but he didn't answer. She left a message. "Kory, this is Tiff. It didn't work, they said no," she cried.

***

Kory was in the shower. When Reesy saw his phone spin on the dresser, she went over and saw Tiffany's name across the screen. She waited until it stopped ringing and went to his call log and deleted the call. When the voice mail notification popped up, she went to his messages and deleted it. She wanted to hear what it said, but couldn't take a chance on him coming out and catching her listening to it. When he came out the shower, she didn't say a word.

Tiffany was glad she had her purse and keys. She went to the parking lot got into her Beemer and left. She drove home in a daze wondering, *What now? One more season and then unemployment.* She walked into her house and went straight for the liquor cabinet. She grabbed the Cîroc and flopped down onto the sofa. After drinking almost half the bottle, she put it down and struggled to get to the bathroom to relieve her bladder. She finished and sat there sobbing.

She couldn't believe they declined. *Why would they decline?* Now, her and her entire staff would have to move on to something else. She stood, peeled off her clothes, and went to bed naked.

The next morning, she woke up and decided she wouldn't allow this to consume her. She called a meeting and gave her staff the farewell speech. She ended it with, "Let's finish this with a bang." They all applauded.

What could she do? It was out of her hands. She had contacted fifteen networks and gotten nowhere, so she accepted it for what it was worth.

Tiffany and Asia arrived on time for Kory and Tressa's engagement party. Tiffany was excited because she was going to see Kennedy. They went inside and the host showed them to their table. They were seated at Kory's family's table right next to Kennedy. She went to the open bar to get a drink and then she saw Kennedy.

She screamed. "Kay, oh my God!"

"Tiffany, how are you?" Kennedy yelled back. They hugged for what seemed like eternity.

"Look at you. You haven't changed a bit."

"You haven't either, girl. You are slaying in that outfit. You are still gorgeous," her friend said.

"And so are you," she said. They heard a voice call out for Kennedy and turned to see who it was. "Oh my God, that is not Cherae," Tiffany said, floored.

"Tiffany?" Cher said.

"Cher," she said and they hugged.

"What are you doing in L.A., girl? And furthermore, why am I not at you and Kory's engagement party? We all know y'all had a thing for each other." She winked.

"We did not," Tiffany, said denying it.

"Ummm, ya did," Cher said and they laughed.

"Well, I heard you dated him," Tiffany said.

"Shhhh, don't you ever repeat that again. That should not have happened at all." They laughed again.

They went to their seats and Kennedy and Tiffany whispered back and forth, catching up and reminiscing.

The DJ came on the mic and got the engagement party started. Tiffany dipped out to the ladies' room, and when she came out she saw him. It was Langley Green. Her feet were like cement, but she decided to approach him.

"Excuse me, Mr. Green," she said.

He looked at her and the person he was speaking to excused himself and moved on. "Yes?" he answered.

"I don't mean to bother you, and I know this is supposed to be a celebration, but I wanted to take a moment to thank you for the opportunity of pitching to your network. I know you declined my show, but I thank you for even letting me in the door. In the future, if you are looking for a young, fresh writer, please keep me in mind," she said humbly.

He frowned. "I'm sorry, young lady, but have we met?"

"No, sir, not formally." She extended her hand. "I'm Tiffany Richardson, executive producer and head writer for the series *Boy Crazy*. Your daughter spoke to you about me a couple weeks ago." The look on his face told her he had no idea what she was talking about. "You set me up with an interview with Wallace Mitchell." He still looked like a deer in headlights. "I'm sorry, sir, you have no idea who I am, do you?"

"No, I'm afraid I don't, but I'd like for you to fill me in really quickly on what I am supposed to have done."

They walked over to a little bench and sat. Tiffany was amazed that he was inclined to hear her out. When she finally paused, he told her that he was familiar with the show and he knew of her and how she had taken the series from number six to number one in just one season. He told her to contact his office on Monday and they'd go from there.

Knowing that Tressa had to be behind her fake meeting with Wallace Mitchell, she begged him not to mention their conversation to her.

She didn't want to cause problems with her and Kory. He assured her that she had nothing to worry about.

They went back to the party. Although she was upset about what Tressa had done, she honestly envied the fact that the other woman had Kory. She told herself that she'd be okay. After Kennedy and Cherae headed back to their hotel, Asia was nowhere to be found. Tiffany texted her and called her, but got no response. She grabbed a glass of champagne from a server's tray and went out to the terrace to take in the beautiful view. If she didn't hear back from Asia soon, she was going to have her paged.

"Are you enjoying the party?" a male voice asked from behind her.

"Yes, it was very nice. Congratulations, Kory," she said, looking out at the city.

"I've been waiting to hear from you so I could congratulate you too," he said.

She turned to look at him. "On what?" she asked, puzzled.

"To congratulate you on your new deal. I was sure you'd heard back from Wallace by now. I tried to ask him earlier, but when I turned around, he was gone."

"I didn't get it," she said sadly, not wanting to tell him that his fiancée lied.

"That's impossible, Tiff, how did you not get it?"

"I don't know, Kory. Wallace called and said my show wasn't a fit. So there, I didn't get it, okay?" She knew then that Tressa must have intercepted her call and message, but it didn't matter. She was Kory's choice. He was going to have to live with that whore-bitch for the rest of his days.

As soon as Darryl had gotten her alone, he filled her in on who Tressa really was, or how she used to be. He told her how she had run through men like water running through a pipe and how many times she had been in and out of rehab, but now she was finally clean, sober, and wife material.

"Tiffany, there is still a chance," Kory said. "I'll talk to Langley myself and maybe he will give you another chance."

For the first time, she felt sorry for him. He was marrying the bitch of L.A., not the queen he thought she was. "Listen, Kory, I don't need anyone else's help. I'm doin' me every single day of my life without the help of others. I will find my own way. It was good seeing you and catching up with you. I hope you and Tressa make each other happy." Teary-eyed, she turned to walk away.

"Tiff, what's this, good-bye?" he asked. She could tell he was confused.

"Yes, Kory, it is. Seeing you again was great, you know, but it was bad timing. I hope things work out for you. Take care." She hurried off.

She dropped the glass trying to put it on the table and ran to the elevator, pressing the button a million times until the doors finally slid open. She stepped in and heard his voice calling her name as they shut. He stood in front of the doors and she caught a glimpse of his beautiful face before they shut completely. She pulled out her phone and tried Asia again. She still couldn't reach her, so she hailed a cab. When they pulled off, she saw Kory running after them, heard him yelling her name, but she instructed the driver to keep going.

Tiffany was confused and didn't understand why things had taken a turn for the worst for her life. She was facing more than a crossroads; it was like a busy intersection that she was afraid to cross, because she knew she'd get hit.

She decided to let it all go. She had made a nice piece of change in the last few years, so money was the least of her worries. She decided she'd focus on the final season, and after that find something new. She scrolled through her phone and deleted Kory from her contacts. She wanted to go on as if she had never run into him that day. He was getting married to the queen bitch of L.A., and she didn't need that kind of drama in her life.

After she paid the cab driver, she went inside and declared that there would be no more tears. She hit the button to turn on her system, went to Fantasia, and cranked "I'm Doin' Me" as she undressed and showered. She kept it on repeat until she was ready to turn in. She got into bed, and her cell phone began to vibrate. She had forgotten to turn the ringer back on when she got home. She looked at it, and when she saw the 773 area code and number, she knew it was Kory, so she hit IGNORE. He called back several times then he sent a text asking her why she wouldn't talk to him. She sat up and looked at the message for a few minutes, and then he was at her door.

Chapter Eleven

Tiffany finally opened the door and let him in. She went over to the sofa and sat and he sat on the ottoman in front of her.

"You know you shouldn't be here," she said, breaking the silence.

"I know," he said with his head down.

"Then why did you come?"

"Honestly, Tiff, I don't know. You stormed out and I don't know what I did to make you so angry with me. I drove here asking myself, 'Why do I even care?'"

"And what did you come up with?" she asked.

He was silent. He wanted to say, "Because I think I'm in love with you," but he knew that would be selfish, because he still loved Tressa. All he knew was he didn't want to lose Tiffany again.

"Tiff, all I can say is I don't want it to be good-bye. I don't know what it is, but since you and I have reconnected, I've been different.

When you're around, I'm happy. I feel like I can just be Kory around you and not pretend or sacrifice what I want so you can be happy. Just say that we can still be friends. That's all I'm asking of you, Tiffany. I don't want to lose touch with you again. Please, Tiff."

"We can't, Kory. And I know what you mean about being different since that day. Kory, I had a major crush on you back in high school. I wanted to be your girl so bad, you know? But you had girls like Charnette Ryan and Porscha Jamison, and then after all these years to hear you even dated Cherae Thompson. I was never in that league, so I didn't qualify. When we met for dinner and I walked up and saw you standing there with Tressa, it was my reality check. Another gorgeous girl I can't compete with. I'm not like those women, and this is not high school. I refuse to sit and watch your fairy tale romance with Tressa. I'm not going to subject myself to envy when it comes to you, so, no, we can't be friends. I want to get back to the life I had before seeing you in that restaurant. I want to put the lid back on these feelings I have for you and get completely over you."

He sat and processed what she said before he replied. "I never knew you felt that way about me, Tiffany. I never knew that you felt like you weren't good enough or pretty enough or that you thought you had to compete. It's true, I like beautiful women. I love gorgeous women, but what you don't know is that you are one of them." She dropped her head really low. "I had feelings for you back then too, Tiffany, and honestly, I thought I wasn't *your* type.

"You ran with the smart kids, and back in high school, I didn't take education that serious. I didn't wise up until I almost flunked out of college. My dad threatened to pull the financial plug on me, so I got by. As I got older, I changed and went back to school for a different degree. For the first time, I applied myself, and I'm who I am because I changed.

"Back then, I had no idea what love was. All I knew is that I loved to be around you and talk to you and the way your breath smelled like grape Now and Laters. When you used to laugh, you'd snort, and I adored that. I went away and you faded further and further into the back of my mind, but the other week, seeing you again, all grown up and sexy and smart and ambitious, those feelings began to resurface. God knows, Tiffany, if I hadda known six months ago that I'd see you again, I would have run the other way from Tressa and waited every day 'til the day I could see you again. But things didn't work out that way.

"I know it's selfish of me to ask you to continue to be a part of my life even though I am getting married and if that makes me a selfish asshole, Tiff, that's what I am." He moved closer to her. "You are beautiful, Tiffany—gorgeous, sexy, and all that, and you don't have to compete with any woman. If things were different, I'd be with you." He touched her lips softly with his.

She closed her eyes. "You should go," she whispered.

"I know," he said before he kissed her again.

"Please, Kory, leave now. This can only lead to my bed, and that would be a bad thing."

"I know, but I want to," he whispered back.

"What about Tressa?" she asked softly and allowed him to kiss her neck.

"I want you, Tiffany," he said. He pushed his tongue into her mouth.

She lay back and he got on top of her. They kissed deeply and he opened her short robe. She wore a sexy nightie and no panties. He slid a strap down and exposed one of her erect nipples to ravish it with his mouth and his cell phone rang.

They both jumped up. Reality. He had to go; what they were doing was so wrong. He looked at the caller ID and held the phone until the ringing stopped.

Tiffany adjusted her gown and closed her robe. "Kory, I need you to go."

He stood up. His phone rang again and he didn't even bother to look at it because he knew it was Tressa. "I'll go, Tiffany, and I'm sorry. I'd never do anything ever to purposely hurt you."

She nodded. "I know, Kory." She walked him to the door and she opened it.

"So this is it?"

"I'm afraid it is," she replied.

He knew there was nothing left to say. He leaned in and kissed her softly on her forehead. "Take care of yourself, Tiffany."

"You too," she said and shut the door.

Kory stood on her porch for a few moments before he headed to his car. He got in and hit the steering wheel because he was so angry. Angry that he was involved with Tressa when he wanted to be with Tiffany. He wanted to make love to her that night and not go home where he had to beg like a dog for some pussy. The passion in Tiffany's kiss was unforgettable. He and Tressa had never shared a kiss like that. Tiff welcomed him with her kiss, and he knew she would have welcomed him inside of her body. He wouldn't have to make deals for it like he did with Tressa. He cranked the engine and considered going home and calling the wedding off. But he didn't want to hurt Tressa like that.

It wasn't her fault that he had recently run into his high school crush. All he could think was, *What am I going to do without her now that I know I could have her?* He thought about turning around and begging Tiffany to have him, but what good would that do if he hadn't broken it off with Tressa? His phone rang again and he hit the Bluetooth button on his dash.

"Yeah," he said, knowing it was Tressa.

"When are you coming home?"

"I'm headed there now," he said.

"And where did you have to go that was so important?"

"Reesy, babe, please. I'm so not in the mood to be badgered. I'll be there soon." He hit the button to end the call.

When he finally made it home, he sat in his car to get his thoughts together before he got out. He didn't want to argue, fuss, or fight. He just wanted to take off that damn tux, shower, and get some sleep. He went inside and found candles lit. *You have got to be kidding me,* he thought. She rarely ever wanted to make love or share an evening of romance, and now all he wanted was to run back to Tiffany's love nest.

Tressa came out in a hot-ass two piece and looked absolutely amazing, but he wasn't interested. She smiled and he just looked at her, but his dick smiled back.

"Hey, sweetie, I wanted to give you your engagement gift," she said, moving close to him.

"And what is that?" he asked.

She took a couple steps back, turned to the side and posed. "Me, of course."

"You know what, Reesy, this day has been overwhelming and busy and nonstop. I'm tired." Even though his body wanted her physically, his mind and heart was still at Tiffany's place.

"Oh, you don't have to do anything," she said, going to grab some wine glasses. "I want to serve you. You know a little sucking and a whole lot of fucking." She handed him a glass and winked. For the first time, he thought she was corny, even a joke.

"Honey, as good as that sounds," he said, putting his glass down, "I'm tired. I'm going to go up and shower and hit the hay." Her head was painful, she couldn't do it worth shit, and he got tired of her test runs on his man. And her sex was, well . . . well, it gave him a nut. He turned to leave the room.

"Hit the hay?" she yelled behind him.

"Yes, Reesy, hit the hay," he repeated.

She followed him up to his room and he started to undress. "Did you fuck her?"

"Fuck who?"

"Don't play fucking games with me, Kory. Tiffany. Did you fuck that bitch?" He just looked at her and continued to undress. "Answer me, motherfucker!" she yelled, getting in his face.

He didn't like that, so it was time to check her. "Okay, let's get this straight right now. I am not one of your groupies or fans. You will not yell at me, question me, or talk to me like you talk to those who kill to be in your presence. As I told you before, Tiffany is a friend. And, no, I did not sleep with her. I am going to shower and then go to bed. If you still want to live it up tonight, I suggest that you get dressed and call your entourage and have a car to pick you up, because I'm not up for your shit tonight."

"Fine!" she said. "I'll see you when I see you." She went to her closet.

Since she couldn't make Kory submit, Tressa decided to go out and kick it with those she could. Her so-called friends were her stepstools. They were always too busy kissing her ass to notice she didn't give a shit. Because she was rich, she didn't have to beg or demand a man to do anything, but that was not the case with Kory. She didn't love him as much as she loved money, and if it weren't for her inheritance, she would have told him that night to kiss her ass. But she didn't want to lose her money. Or her man to a loser like Tiffany. Miss Tiffany was a threat, and she wasn't going to let a runner-up snatch up her goods.

Chapter Twelve

The next morning, the ringing phone woke Tiffany and she turned over and scrambled for it. When she finally retrieved it, the ringing stopped, so she put it on the other pillow. She had a terrible headache. After Kory had walked out of her life for good the night before, she opened a bottle of pinot and drank the entire bottle. Wine headaches were the worst and she knew she'd have to sleep that one off. Two minutes later, the phone rang again and she grabbed it. It was Darryl.

"Dee, why so early?" She closed her eyes.

"Honeycomb, it is a quarter 'til one. What kept you in bed so late, Miss Thang?"

"Pinot. What's up?"

"Well, the buzz is your star child, Jennifer, aka Claire, has a new boo and his name is Wade Simmons."

Her eyes popped opened. "Wade Simmons, as in L.A. Lakers Wade Simmons?"

"Yep, and since she couldn't reach you last night, Miss Pinot, she called *moi* and asked if there was a way to write him into an episode or two."

Tiffany was awake now and somehow her headache disappeared. "Shut the front door," she said, mimicking him.

"Exactly. So, I've been bouncing around ideas all morning in my head. What if we have him come in as the new basketball coach for Hampton High? And if we can get him to appear on at least five episodes, we can write him in."

"Okay, that sounds good, but he's her new boo, why would he do that? And not only that, how much is that gonna cost the network? You know they have a tight grip on our budget."

"Well, there is more, love bug."

Tiffany wondered why he had a nickname for everyone under the sun. "Give me the more." She got up and went to the bathroom; her bladder was about to burst.

"Turns out that he is not her new boo; he's been her boo for eight months. They just had to keep their thing on the low until his wife signed the papers."

"That's right," she said. "He was going through a divorce."

"And here is where you would kiss me if we were in the same room."

She doubted that. "Give. Come on, Dee, you are so dramatic," she said getting up and flushing. She went to the sink to wash her hands then headed toward the kitchen.

"Yes, I am, hello," he said. She could see him in her mind, standing with his hand on his hip. "Enteeeway," he continued, "since he is also on a crusade to help save her show, he has agreed to do it for free."

Tiffany screamed. She just may have kissed him if they were in the same room.

"Is that not like the best news on this Sunday morning?" he said.

"Oh my God, Dee, get dressed. I'm going to call Myah. We are going in on a Sunday. We cannot waste any time. Myah has to get an agreement typed right away and we have to shoot out some new ideas and get some rewrites going." She went back to her room and into her walk-in and then it hit her. "Dee, when is the next happening event?" she asked. Darryl was up on everything. He was her *TMZ*.

"Ummm, if I'm not mistaken, Clover Winters is having a charity event to support battered women next Saturday."

"Okay. I know you got the hookup, right?"

"Of course. But . . ."

"But what?"

"Why are we attending?"

"Ummm, duh. Clover is like one of Hollywood's biggest actors, and actors support actors."

"Sweet pea, I still don't follow."

"Actors support actors. If we can get in a room full of actors, we may be able to sway some of the heavy hitters to make a guest appearance. You know, appear as a substitute teacher, a guidance counselor, or a new cashier at the girls' hangout. We can get a guest to play a new mean-ass cashier the girls scheme to get fired or something. Joy's mom is single; soon-to-be single this season. A guest star to be a date from hell would be hilarious." Ideas popped into her head left and right.

"Oh my Gucci, you are a genius, Tiff. Get your ass in gear and make sure you grab your re-corder, because when ideas pop up in your head, they need to be noted."

"Yes, and with the right celebrity guest, we can maybe reach a broader audience."

Her spinning with possibilities, she got off the phone so she could shower. She wanted to get into the idea room and toss around ideas and alternative shows in case they managed to land some celebrities to make guest appearances. In all the excitement, she forgot about her heartache from Kory and her headache from the pinot.

She showered and put on a sundress and wedges. It was Sunday, so she didn't have to look the part that day. She just wanted to go in and get some work in. On the way to the office, she stopped at the local grocery store, ran to the deli, and selected three premade trays: one fruit, one veggie, and one assorted meat and cheese. She tried to resist the wing platter, but snatched one up anyway. They had a microwave, so why not? She strolled to the liquor section and grabbed three reds, three whites, and three sparkling wines. She knew Brad was a beer man, so she grabbed a case of Bud Light and went to the checkout.

When she arrived, she called Myah and told her to send a couple people down to help her with the things she purchased. They set the food up on the buffet table that sat along the wall and everyone pulled out their electronic devices and went to their show's program and got to work. They came up with six alternate episode ideas, hoping they could put a celebrity guest in that role.

Satisfied with the day of work with her favorite team, she wanted to head home, but Asia called and asked her to meet her for dinner. She didn't want to go, but she agreed to meet her at Sunset Towers restaurant and bar. When she arrived, her friend came over and greeted her with a hug and kiss.

"Hey, girl, don't you look cute in your peach dress?" Asia said.

"And you too in your white," Tiffany said.

They were seated and started chatting. Tiffany wondered why Asia kept holding up her left hand when she spoke. She finally noticed a ring on her fourth finger. "Asia, tell me that is not a diamond." She hadn't known she and her Rude Boy was that serious. She thought their relationship was more sexual than mental.

"Yes, Edward asked me this morning," she said beaming.

"Edward as in the Edward you just met at Kory's a few weeks ago?" Tiffany was shocked.

"Yes." Asia's smile was wider than an airplane runway.

"And you said yes? You've known him for like five minutes, Asia." Tiffany wasn't smiling. She thought this was a major rush.

"You don't have to know someone long, Tiffany, to know you are in love," she explained. "Edward and I are each other's match."

"How do you know that, Asia? You can't possibly know enough about him in this short time to share the rest of your life with him," Tiffany said trying to make sense of it, but she could see that she was upsetting her friend.

"Listen, Tiffany, I am an adult, okay, and I can make decisions for myself. I thought you, of all people, would understand." Asia waved for the server to order a drink.

Tiffany was incredulous. "Why would you think that? How did you think for a second that I'd understand that you are in love with a man in a shorter time than it takes me to dry my hair?"

"Because you've only known Kory just as long and you're in love with him."

Tiffany laughed. "Asia, listen to yourself. I've known Kory over fifteen years."

"No, you met him over fifteen years ago and haven't seen him since. He is just as much a stranger to you as Edward is to me."

Tiffany knew that in a way, Asia was right. It was a stretch of reasoning, but she was right.

"Asia, the point is I fell in love with Kory back then," she said in her defense. "And over the years, I've always loved him."

"But you loved a boy back then. For crying out loud, you were a damn teen. This man is not that boy anymore. You haven't even spent as much time with him as I've spent with Edward the last few weeks and you know you love him, so why can't I love Edward?"

Tiffany decided to leave it at that. "You know what, Asia, I'm sorry, okay? Congratulations," she said sincerely. "And I'm sorry for reacting that way."

"Yuh should be," Asia said and smiled. "Yuh di first person mi tell, and yuh come rain pon mi parade."

The server finally came over to take their drink orders. They ordered and ended up sharing an appetizer because they were not too hungry. They finished and stood outside for a moment before they parted.

"Again, I'm happy for you, Asia," Tiffany said, "and I wish the best for you, girl. Come here." She hugged her tight. "I love you, girl, so much." She meant it.

There was no schedule on love and that made Tiffany question her love for Kory. Maybe she didn't love him. Maybe she was just caught up in the memories and it was meant to be just the way it was: him with Tressa and her with someone else, hopefully soon.

"Mi love yuh too, gal," she said.

They said good night and Tiffany drove home telling herself she would get over Kory and just focus on her career and job situation. She had to make some long-term decisions and some short-term goals to get over this obstacle in her life. When she got home, she made the call she had put off all day. She had to call her best friend, Rose, and tell her that she and Kory meeting again wasn't destiny. It was just another bag that she needed to finally unpack and stop carrying around on her trips of love.

Chapter Thirteen

The network wasn't impressed at all. Rather, Mr. Keiffer wasn't impressed with all the guest star appearances Tiffany managed to land. He looked at her with the same dull-ass expression he had before she told him the lineup for the show. She was bursting with excitement and so were her cast and crew. They were only days away from rehearsals. She managed to get Brandy Norwood, Terri Ellis, Meagan Good, Mo'Nique, Pooch Hall, and a couple newcomers to commit to the show.

She had such a great conversation with Tisha Campbell-Martin and Tichina Arnold that she came up with a concept right then and there on the spot for them to appear together on the show. She had a vision of Shana's mom getting together with her old high school group and they decide to sing for a charity event and everyone wants to be the lead. She envisioned them being on stage singing at the top of their

lungs trying to outsing each other. Shana's
mom, Rita, on the show had a singing voice, but
since the show was based on the girls so much,
their parents were not in the forefront. Now, it
was everyone's chance to have a title episode in
this last season.

"So, Mr. Keiffer," she said, "you are welcome
to come to our tapings. Bill never missed one."

"If I have time." He didn't even look up. He
continued to give his undivided attention to the
papers on his desk.

She knew that meant "make your exit," so she
stood. "Okay, Mr. Keiffer, I'll leave you to it." He
still didn't look up.

She went down the hall and hit the elevator
button to go back down to her floor. She made
it to her floor and when she got closer to her
office, she realized she had her notes, but not
her phone. It must have fallen when she was
going through her notes to bring Mr. Keiffer
up to speed on where the show was going.
She went back up to look for it. His door was
cracked a little, and she could hear his voice,
so she knew he was in. She raised her arm to
knock, but stopped when she overheard that
word. The word she still used from time to
time, but not for the same reasons.

"Yes, you heard me right," she heard him say. "There is no way in hell I'm going to let a pack of *niggers* have the number one spot at my station. When my family first started this network, the only thing *niggers* did was clean the place. When Billy took charge, he started hiring *niggers* left and right." He chuckled. "Then I learn he gave executive control of the show to this *nigger*. He must have lost his damn mind. When I heard that, I knew I had to shut it down. Even if they rewrite the entire season giving me what I demanded, I will let her know the offer no longer stands. Either way, I'm not renewing their contract."

Tiffany was floored. He was an old-ass racist. It wasn't that he didn't think the show was great. He didn't like the fact of it being a black show. She backed away from the door.

"Don't cry, Tiffany, don't you cry," she instructed herself. She pressed the button over and over again until the doors finally opened. She rushed to her office and shut the door behind her quickly. She leaned back against it, slid down the door to the floor, and sobbed. She couldn't believe it. Out of all the reasons for him to want them gone. Racist. He was an old-ass, racist bastard. She took a few deep breaths and wanted to scream.

When she was able, she got up and went to her desk, flopped down in her chair, opened her drawer, and grabbed her Remy. She dumped the unfinished coffee that was in her cup into the trash and grabbed her unused napkins from her desk to wipe the cup out. She poured herself more than a shot's worth, took a couple swallows, and caught her breath.

There was a tap on her door. She wiped her face real good and said, "Come in." It was Myah.

"Hey, Mr. Keiffer sent this down. Said you left it in his office." She handed Tiffany her phone. She looked at her boss closely. "Tiff, what's wrong?" She sat down in the chair across from her.

"Close the door, Mee-Mee," Tiffany said.

Myah rushed over and shut it. "Tiff, what is it?" She came back and sat down. "What happened in the meeting with Keiffer?"

"He's shutting the show down because he's a racist." Tiffany blinked back her tears. "He is a fucking racist, Mee-Mee." She grabbed a Kleenex.

"How do you know that, Tiffany? What would make you think something so terrible about him?"

"I heard him, he said the word 'nigger' loud and fucking clear. I heard him on the phone. It doesn't matter what direction I take the show in, he still would have not renewed our contract."

"Whoa, Tiffany, that's messed up. What are you going to do?"

"What can I do, quit? I should just quit and walk away from this stupid-ass network."

"And give him the satisfaction of shutting you down? You are a hellava producer and a kick-ass writer. If you just quit and walk away now, he wins. Screw him, Tiffany, screw this network. You end this like you said you would and move on. This season is going to be so kick-ass he is going to be begging you to come back. Not one show in this network's history has ranked higher than *Boy Crazy*, so don't you dare think about quitting."

"You know what, Myah, you are right. I just have to give up this hope of him seeing what a huge mistake it is to let *Boy Crazy* go. He doesn't want us here. He doesn't want to sit back and watch his white shows get stomped by our show. It's a no-win situation and I am fine with that. I had a great show and it's been a great run. KCLN is just a stepping stone. After this season, I'm sure someone will hire me, even if it's for a new show."

Myah nodded and smiled. "Yes, that is the truth." She stood to leave and paused. "Tiffany, one more thing?"

"Yes, what's up?"

"When the show is done and you guys are gone, I hope you won't be upset with me if I stay on. I know Keiffer is a racist bastard, but I have three kids, Tiffany, and this job has benefits." Her words came out in a nervous rush. "I may have to stick around here after you guys are gone."

"Myah, that is fine. Why would you think for a second that I wouldn't understand? You have to do what's best for your family, and I wouldn't blame you if you kept your position here."

"Thanks, Tiffany. Truth, you are the best boss I've had since I've worked here and when it's all said and done, I am going to miss you."

Tiffany stood and went around to hug her. "Just promise me that I will be able to take you with me if I land something new. I'll make sure you get benefits for your babies," she promised.

"No doubt. I'd be outta here before Alice in editing could finish her dozen donuts." Alice was a heavyset woman who loved donuts. If Myah didn't snatch one in the morning before nine, at least twelve of the good ones would have been eaten by her colleague.

"Great. Now, order everyone's favorite Chinese and have it delivered. We only have four days before rehearsals begin. You know the season comes on us quicker than Alice hits those donuts." They laughed.

"Sure, I'm on it. And, Tiffany, you are fabulous. This network is going to regret letting you go."

Tiffany smiled. "Thank you, Mee-Mee."

When her assistant was on the other side of the door, Tiffany sat back at her desk and finished her drink. She swallowed it slowly and then she noticed the light blinking on her cell phone. She picked it up to check it and saw that it was a text:

I just wanted 2 say hi N I hope U R well.

Even though she had deleted his number from her phone, she recognized the number. She stared at it for a moment and then tossed her phone back on the desk. "Please, Kory, just let me be," she said out loud.

It had been a little less than two weeks since they had fooled around on her sofa. Every time her mind tried to replay the scene, she'd moved to something else. She hated daydreaming because she always let her mind wander off to Koryland when she just wanted to forget him.

"Asia's right, I have no idea who you are now. We're not kids anymore," she said and took the last swallow of the remaining Remy that was in her cup. She grabbed her tablet and headed to the idea room.

The following week, they were on the set for rehearsal of the first episode, "Meet the Teacher." In that episode, Wade Simmons made his debut. Even though he didn't have any acting experience, he did a good job and they were ready to record.

Sometimes, scenes took several shoots to get it right, and since every scene was recorded separately and at different times, she put in more hours. After the first episode was recorded, she stayed late to make sure things were good. She was leaving the studio a little later than usual when she saw a familiar face walking toward the trailer of another big-shot actor. She focused a little more and wondered what Tressa was doing with Stephen Willis at that time of night. She wondered if she was still with Kory and if he knew she was arm-in-arm with that arrogant bastard. It wasn't her business or her concern, so she dismissed what she saw and headed to her car.

When she got home, she remembered Keith, and even though it was late, she called him.

"Hey," he said.

"Keith, I'm sorry I'm calling so late. How are you?"

"I'm good, Tiff, how are you? Long time, no hear."

"Yeah, well I've been dealing with my show."

"I thought it was because you wanted to avoid any conversations about Kory," he joked.

"Yeah, that too, but the reason why I was calling is I wanted to confirm Julia's number," she lied. "We are taping now and I want to confirm that she'll still be a part of the show." He gave her the number again and she wanted to ask about Kory, but resisted. "Thanks so much, Keith."

"So are you going to attend the wedding?"

"Nah, I don't think that would be a good idea."

"I understand. I still wonder 'til this day why is he still going through with it. But hey, not my life, right?"

"Right," Tiffany said. "We gotta let grown folks do what they do."

"Indeed. However, I would like for you to still hang out with me. I want you to meet my wife and not be a stranger."

"Will do, Keith, I promise. I want to meet her too."

"Well, keep in touch, and I promise, no Kory talk if that's what you want."

"That's what I need," she corrected him.

"Okay, Tiff, I gotta run. Time to get my kids to bed."

"Okay, Keith. I will see you soon," she said and hung up.

It was confirmed, the wedding was still on. Why Tressa was at Stephen's trailer at nine at night should not have been her concern, but she knew exactly who to go to for answers.

Chapter Fourteen

The next couple of weeks flew by and recordings went great. Finally, it was the day that Julia Valentine was to be on set. Everyone and their momma showed up just to hear her sing. Her voice was like no other, and when it was time for her scene, the entire set lapsed into silence. This was the episode where Claire's father died and she sang at his funeral. Timothy Warren, in the role of Claire's father, had found a new home and would be leaving the show whether or not the contract was renewed. He tragically died in an accident at his construction site, and although this was make-believe, there were no dry eyes when Julia finished her song.

When the day was done, Tiffany rushed over to thank the singer for participating and being a part of her show. "Julia, oh my God, you were phenomenal. I thank you so much for doing this. This episode should have been the show's finale."

Julia smiled. "You are so very welcome. Anything for Keith. You know he helped to save my family's lives?"

Tiffany didn't know the entire story. "Somewhat, yes, only what I read."

"Well, he came through for me and I will always come through for him . . . and Kory." She gave her a look, but she ignored it.

"Well, thanks again, Julia," Tiffany said, hoping she'd drop the conversation about Kory.

"You're welcome. And, I will add that he is marrying the wrong one. I'm not an expert, but I have ears, and when the fellas are together, you're Kory's number one topic, not Tressa." She winked. "By the way, we are having a birthday party at my house for my li'l Juliana and I would love for you to come. You know, rub elbows with some people. This show is a great show, and I know a few people who you may want to meet. Their children are on the guest list. I will definitely promote the show and tell all of my fans to tune in."

Tiffany accepted the invite and when Julia left, Tiffany called Asia to invite her, but she said she was going to be out of town meeting Edward's folks.

when we started taping, I came out
ressa going to Stephen's trailer. Now
here watching them whisper back and
each other's ear. Am I overreacting, or
tect affair?"

honeydew, you are not overreacting,
r, boop, ummm, no!"

what could it be? People don't be up on
her like that unless there is something
n."

I think you're right, honey bun. Affair, no,
ke, maybe."

e was shocked. "Drugs, no way. She is
osed to be clean. Kory would never marry a
head."

ell, that is the only thing I can think of.
phen likes to swing on poles, FYI, and I
w he ain't tapping that. Everybody in the gay
mmunity knows that Stephen don't like cat."

But, he is, like, the sexiest motherfucker on
levision now," she said in disbelief. "Women
re all over him."

"And that is for image only. Trust, pee-wee is
ay," Darryl said, holding up his pinky finger.

"Nooooo. You hooked up with him?"

"Good girls don't tell," he said and she burst
into laughter.

She put her phone in her pocket, disappointed, and then she spotted Darryl. He was gay, yes, but also a social butterfly and an elbow-rubber. She walked over and told him about the party. When she said at Julia's house, he practically leaped into her arms

A few days later, they arrived and waited for the valet to park their car.

"Look at this, Tiffany, this is how I want to live," Darryl said, looking at the enormous lot that Julia's mansion sat on.

"You and me both," Tiffany said. "If I can just sell one of my manuscripts, it would be on from then on."

Darryl turned to her with his eyebrows raised. "You have manuscripts, buttercup?"

"Yes, I am a writer, Dee, that's what I do. I have more than sitcom goals, you know." The valet opened her door for her to get out.

"Hey, I ain't hatin'," he said and got out.

They entered the party and mingled. There were several celebrities they had never met, and Tiffany had to hold Darryl back at times and remind him not to act like a groupie.

After a while, she saw them. Kory and Tressa walked out to the party tent hand-in-hand and her heart dropped. She knew he'd probably be there, but she thought she'd be able to handle seeing the two of them. She kept her distance, but before long, Kory spotted her and made his way over. When Darryl saw him approaching, he went MIA.

"Tiff, how nice to see you," he said.

She smiled. "Hi, Kory, nice to see you too." Her heart thumped. She really was happy to see him.

"How are things? I heard your show is going to be a series to remember and Julia tore the house down the other day." He took a sip of the drink he held.

"Yes, I think we are going to do very well. I mean, my team is awesome. The cast is at the top of their game. From makeup to wardrobe, this is the best season thus far."

"That's great, and I am so sorry you didn't get the contract at TiMax. I thought for sure it was yours."

"No worries, it is what it is right?" she said. She saw Tressa approaching.

"Kory, darling, I need you. I have someone I want you to meet." She pulled his arm, urging him away. "Oh, hi," she said as if she'd just seen Tiffany. She gave him another tug. "Come on, babe, I need to introduce you to someone."

Tiffany watched a[...] dragged off, his eyes [...] fiancée pulled him w[...] over to another couple[...] to the introduction, bu[...] her. She moved around[...] to get his gorgeous face [...] was too late. Seeing him[...] found Darryl and he caugh[...] celeb connections he made,[...] wouldn't be out of work for lo[...]

The party transitioned fr[...] to an evening adult soiree a[...] glad she and Darryl stuck arou[...] was gone and the child festiviti[...] away. The bars went up and the[...] were loaded with adult food. Tif[...] pressed. She and Darryl sat in a[...] chair recliners and gossiped about[...] who was with whom. Tiffany spotte[...] and in a matter of seconds, Tressa v[...] to him like glue. She saw them whis[...] and forth and then they eased away t[...] Tiffany knew there was something go[...] now, but what? She decided to ask he[...] source.

"So, Dee, don't think this question is prov[...] by jealousy, because that's not the case. A co[...]

"Bitch, please, you're as bad as they come," she said playfully.

"Yeah, you're right," he confirmed. "Just trust me. Stephen is a powdered-nose whore, and if she is tight with him, she is powdering hers too."

Tiffany wanted to run to Kory and tell him. She wanted to give him the heads-up. Darryl seemed to know what she was thinking.

"No, no, no, watermelon," he said. "You will not be the morning news. You will stay out of it. If you run blabbing your mouth, she is going to deny it and act like you are trying to move in. You don't want Kory to think you're trying to abolish his relationship with accusations that his fiancée is a cokehead."

"I don't see it as blabbing, Dee," she protested. "Kory is my friend, and he should know who he is marrying."

"Well, let the cokeheads stand up, because that addiction is not going to stay a secret for long, trust me. Just stay out of it, Tiff, and if and when he does find out, he will be all yours."

Tiffany disagreed, but she didn't dispute his advice. She didn't want to make waves, so she promised Darryl she wouldn't say anything to Kory. But he didn't say anything about talking to Keith.

She hung around a little while longer and as she was about to make her exit, Kory called out her name.

"Yes," she said turning to face him.

"You're leaving?"

"Yeah, it's late and I'm tired."

"Can I walk you out?" he offered.

"Yeah, sure," she said and smiled. They walked toward the door.

"Listen, Tiff, I have tried to respect your wishes and give you your space, but I think about you constantly and I miss you," he said and she was touched. Darryl bumped her arm and gave her a look before walking ahead.

"I miss you too, Kory, but this is for the best," she said.

"The best for who? I thought I meant something to you."

"You do, Kory, and that's the problem." She looked away.

He turned her to face him. "Why can't we just be friends like we were back in school?"

"Because back then, I was able to hide my feelings and not act on them. Now, I am a grown woman with needs, Kory. I can't play around with you and crack jokes like we used to do when we were teens. If you are in my life, I want you to be my man and not just my friend."

Her car pulled up and she went to get into the driver's seat. He stood there and watched her. As she pulled off, she heard Tressa yelling for him. She sounded drunk.

When Tiffany dropped Darryl off, she promised him again that she wouldn't put Tressa and her drug habit into Kory's ear. She would keep that vow, but she knew she was going to put the information into his cousin's ear.

Chapter Fifteen

Kory sat and watched the MMA fight, trying to process the information Keith put on him about Tressa using drugs. Since she and he had decided to live apart until the wedding, he didn't see her as much as he wanted to anymore. She always had wedding stuff going on or plans with her friends. He had noticed a change in her behavior, but he thought it was because of the stress of the wedding planning. It was like she had a split personality at times. One minute she was super nice and mellow, the next she was acting erratic. He tried to give her space because he had no idea what wedding planning was like, but for her to be using drugs didn't sit right with him. He prayed it wasn't true. Yes, she was beginning to drink a little more than she normally did, but she had promised him she'd never touch drugs again.

"How do I confront her?" he had asked Keith during their phone conversation.

"I'm not sure, cuz. I suggest you just pay attention to her and the company she keeps. I heard the person you need to worry about is that Stephen guy."

Kory wondered where he got his info. "Where did you hear this? I thought you said you weren't up on celeb gossip."

"Well, let's just say a friend of mine heard some things and thought you should know."

He knew it could only be one person. "Tiffany?" he asked.

"No, not Tiffany," Keith said.

Kory knew he was lying. "Then who? Who? Who do you know that would be concerned about me and my fiancée?"

"Look, someone we know knows she is hanging with Stephen a lot, and they know he is a cokehead. So since you are the only one who didn't know, I'm telling you to check up on your lady. We both know that Tressa has a past with drugs, Kory. She's been in and out of rehab over the years and she may be using again."

"I know she has a past, cuz, but she has changed. So fucking what if Stephen is a cokehead? That . . . that doesn't mean Reesy is using. She promised me, man, and I believe her."

"Okay, I'll leave it alone. But as your cousin and best friend, I had to say something."

"Well, thank you, but I got this," Kory said and hung up.

He told himself that that wasn't true about Tressa. He knew she changed and he also knew she was on the road to happy. She promised him that she was done with that lifestyle and he believed her. He decided to ignore Keith's accusations and not even entertain his theory. He knew Tressa had a past, but he felt that everyone deserved a second, third, even fourth chance.

He knew it was Tiffany who said that horrible shit about Tressa and he wondered how she could stoop that low, to call his fiancée a coke head. He dialed Tressa's number, wondering how Tiffany could be so jealous that she would say such a horrible thing.

"Hello," she answered.

"Hey, babe, what are you up to?"

"About to hit the strip. I'm ready to party," she screamed.

Kory didn't want to hear that. He wanted to see her. "Why don't you come over and let me run you a bath, pour you a glass of champagne, and make love to you. I've been trying to see you all week long. Your man is missing you."

"Awww, come on, Kory, don't call and fuckin' sour my mood. I am feeling good, and right now, I want to hit L.A. and party, not lay up and cuddle."

"Reesy, I haven't seen you all week. It's always the wedding this, Stephen this, or 'I got plans.' When are you gonna fit me into your plans, babe? I miss you; don't you miss me?"

He heard her blow out a breath of air. "Yes, Kory," she said. "I do, but I already made plans with my girls. I'll tell you what, I'll go out for a couple hours and come back to your place and let you have your way with me."

He smiled. "Okay, that's a bet. Just please, Reesy, be a woman of your word. The last couple times, you were a no-show. Your man is horny. My dick is harder than a slow kid trying to learn algebra." She burst into laughter, but he was serious. He couldn't go another night without sex.

"Okay, nasty boy, by one a.m., I'm there."

He let her go on her word, happy that he was going to be able to bust one. He was never the one to masturbate, so he was looking forward to her visit.

He lay down to wait for her. When he woke up, it was eight a.m. He realized he had fallen asleep waiting for Reesy to show up. He still had his phone in his hand from the night before. After a few drinks of Scotch and Coke, he had begun to text her back to back. He looked at some of the text messages he sent, the last one at three thirty asking her why. He wanted to know why she was doing him the way she was, when she claimed to love him so much. He scrolled through his phone and saw that she had finally texted him back after four saying she wasn't going to make it. He tossed his phone, went to the bathroom, and then went downstairs and got the Sunday paper. He was surprised to see Tiffany on the front page.

The headline read BOY CRAZY'S FINAL SEASON. He sat and read the story of how Tiffany Richardson, born and raised on the south side of Chicago, came to L.A. with dreams of becoming an anchor woman or radio personality, but had walked into the wrong room and landed a job as a writer for the show *Boy Crazy*. He read on to learn that she took the lead by pulling the show from the number six slot to number one in just one season and found herself being promoted to executive producer and head writer for the show in less than two years. The paper expressed how sorry they were to see the show come to an end. They had a Q&A with Tiffany being positive and saying she was confident it wasn't the end.

Kory smiled. He was proud of her and wished she was his fiancée. He knew she would have shown up the night before if she said she would, not like Tressa's busy, lying ass. He knew Tiffany would have put his needs first, before her friends and the night life. Tressa was addicted to the life. She was a rich, spoiled brat, and she loved the fact that L.A. loved her.

When she and Kory were out together, they never paid for anything. Everything was always on the house wherever they went. L.A. loved Tressa and Tressa loved L.A. Sometimes, he felt that she loved L.A. more than she loved him, and he now wondered why she was marrying him. He decided he'd call the person who was closest to her. He wanted someone to tell him the truth. Was she using him or did she love him? He knew Amber was the only one who was sincere enough to tell him the truth.

He called and left her a message and then he called Langley Green. It was a long shot, since Tressa had already asked, but he had to try asking him again. He'd beg if had to, because Tiffany deserved a chance.

Chapter Sixteen

Tiffany's limo pulled up and she got out and walked the red carpet at *Boy Crazy*'s premiere party. Since this was their final season, they decided to go all out and the party was ten times larger than the previous years. She was dressed to kill in a stunning backless red dress, with sparkling diamond accessories and her diamond-studded shoes. She took her time posing for all the cameras, hating that she was single with no one on her arm. She'd normally be dating somebody around season premiere time, but not this time. This year, she was solo.

Party attendees enjoyed cocktails and hors d'oeuvres before they were moved to the media room to watch the season's first episode of the show. It was an hour long and when the credits began, people were on their feet applauding.

The show was a hit and those who had viewed the first episodes commented that they couldn't comprehend why the show was ending. Tiffany glowed with pride when she heard them say the cast was fresh and beautiful and the writers kicked ass on the new season. This season would be funny, sexy, emotional, and witty, with a lot of chemistry and the viewers were going to be in for a treat.

Tiffany wanted to inform the show's supporters during her speech that the network was now run by one of the biggest racists on the planet, but she held her head high and said great things about the network and thanked them for giving her a chance to be a part of their team. She gave a personal thanks to William Keiffer, the network's true owner, and Todd Daniels, the man who had given her Tracy's position. She thanked her cast and crew individually and begged anyone she forgot to mention to forgive her. After they allowed the main cast members and a few others to speak, the party began. Tiffany was tired of greeting and talking, but she kept up her appearance, praying that the night would end soon, because her feet were aching.

She was out on the terrace, taking in the lovely view, when she heard someone behind her clear their throat. She turned around.

"Do you mind if I join you?" the man asked. He walked over with a glass of champagne in his hand for her.

"Don't mind at all, Mr. Grant," she replied and took the glass. Colby Grant was not a newcomer to L.A. His last role on the big screen attracted more success than any other in his entire fourteen-year career. He was so hot that scripts were coming at him left and right since that movie. He was on the list with Denzel, Will, and Blair now. And he was just as fine, she thought.

"What a vast night it has been for you," he said.

"Yes, you can say that. Everything was spectacular, but sadly, this is the end of the road."

"So sorry. I mean, I didn't catch a lot of episodes of your show, but the ones I did manage to catch were great."

"Thank you. Maybe if I could have gotten you on as a guest star, the network would have reconsidered our contract." She smiled.

"Maybe. You never know." He smiled back.

"Well, it's a bittersweet moment, I'll tell you. I'm proud of myself for the success the show had, but I'm so disappointed to have a great run with KCLN and then just get cut from the team.

"Just think of it as a stepping stone. It took me fourteen years, twenty-one movies, and God only knows how many roles as a nobody to finally get here. To get the starring role for *Enlisted* was a dream come true, but most importantly, a blessing from God. You've done so much in so little time, Tiffany, so you're one of the lucky ones. It's just time to move on to the next thing."

"That's just it. I don't have the next thing planned. I was just so confident that KCLN would renew that I didn't plan for the next thing."

"Well then, the next thing is prayer. You just pray and wait."

She looked at him. His eyes were so sincere and he seemed to be more of a gentleman than she thought he'd be. Fine and yet humble was a rare thing in L.A. "Yes," she agreed. "I guess you're right."

"Of course I am. Now, you are going to put on a happy face and come inside and dance with me." He held out an arm and she slid her arm into it.

Her feet were hurting like hell, but how could she deny him? They danced a couple songs, and when the music slowed for the next one, he didn't let her leave the dance floor. She tried to refuse him, to say no, but he wouldn't hear of it and pulled her close.

When the song was over, Tiffany really wanted to leave because her feet felt like they had been hammered by a sledgehammer. She told Colby she was going to call it a night.

"Already? It's not even midnight," he said looking at his watch.

"I know, but my feet are killing me and I want to get out of this dress." She didn't want to be tacky and take off her shoes there. There were still press and media outside.

"I'll tell you what, let me take you home and you change and we can go listen to some jazz. I won't keep you out too late." He flashed his gorgeous smile again.

"Okay, that sounds like a plan. I'll have to let my driver know that it is okay for him to leave."

Colby walked her out. She took a couple more photos alone and a couple with him. She wondered what the tabloids would say about them. She really didn't care because he was fine and living large, so if they assumed he was her man, she didn't see how that could be a bad thing.

They made it to her place and she invited him in while she changed. He took a seat and when she came out in her jeans and halter, he said, "I feel overdressed. Maybe I should change." They both laughed.

"Yes, maybe," she said.

"How about this: we go to my place and just have a couple drinks there, and I'll play you some jazz?"

Tiffany was a little hesitant, but she agreed. They left and drove out to his home. They went inside and he showed her to the patio. She took a seat while he started the fire pit and then ran inside to get her a Chardonnay. He turned on some soft music and went to change. He came back in some long shorts and a tank with his Nike slippers and socks. He joined her and took a sip of his drink. They made small talk, and she started to feel a little attraction between them.

"So what happened between you and your girlfriend? I mean, y'all were together since forever."

"We had about five and a half years, but what the world doesn't know is that damn girl was crazy. I mean, Jasmine was gorgeous, talented, and smart, but had a mad crazy temper. I used to be able to deal with it, you know, but then a year ago, she'd go into these violent rages and things started to get physical. The night of the premiere of *Enlisted*, there was a lot of focus on me and I was being pulled in every direction. As you know in this biz, it's groupie territory, but Jasmine did not want to see women in my face at all. Long story short, I'm like partying, doing the damn thing, and this chick wanted me to sign her tit. So I grabbed her tit with one hand and signed with the other. Jasmine saw it, walked up on me, and slapped the shit outta me in front of everybody. Tiffany, I was so mad and embarrassed, but all I could do was walk out of my own party.

"I left and went home. And when she came home, I told her to get her shit and get out. We broke up for a couple weeks, I calmed down, and let her come home. After that, she became this abusive bitch. She thought she could hit me whenever she was pissed. Things got so bad I had to call the cops on her, and that last time, I pressed charges. I couldn't take it anymore. I had to leave her alone before one of us ended up seriously hurt, because that last time, I hit her back. And I vowed to never hit a woman. That's what happened with Jasmine, and it's been maybe seven or eight months since I saw her last."

"Wow that is crazy. That is one thing I don't condone, hitting. I learned a long time ago not to give a lick if you can't receive a lick. So I keep my hands to myself." She finished that last swallow in her glass.

"Would you like another?"

"Yes, but only one. I think I'm about to hit my limit."

He got up to refill her glass and when he came back, they talked for hours. Before she knew it, it was after five.

"How about I show you around?" he offered.

She nodded yes. He started outside where they were and took her through another entrance from the patio that wrapped around, what seemed to Tiffany, the entire exterior of the house. They finally finished the tour in his master bedroom, and went out onto his huge balcony that over-looked the entire back of the house and from where she could see the city lights.

"Now this is how I planned to live one day," she said out loud.

"Yes, it is nice. I wasn't able to purchase this place until last year, and I'll be here for a while," he said and smiled.

"A while in this place is not a bad idea," she said.

He moved closer to her and embraced her from behind. "You can stay if you'd like. No strings, no requirements, and I promise to stay on my side of the bed."

She knew she should have gone home, but she was enjoying him and his company. "I'll stay if you promise to keep your hands to yourself and don't try no touchy-feely when I close my eyes. Men are bad for that."

"I promise," he said holding up his hands in mock of surrender.

"I'm serious, Colby. If I feel a hand on my breast or my ass, I will take a cab. I promise you I will."

"I'll sleep in the chair if you want me to," he said and smiled.

"No, I want to lie with you," she said and they both smiled. He leaned in and gave her a soft kiss and she let him.

"Well, shall we?" he asked.

They went into his bedroom and he gave her a T-shirt to sleep in. She went into the master bathroom to change and walked back out with her clothes in her hand.

"You can lay your things there," he said, pointing to a plush chair in a corner of the room. "I'm going to go down and lock up."

While he was gone, she pulled back the covers and climbed into his huge bed. When he came back, he got in with her, still wearing his shorts and tank, and he grabbed the remote. He lowered the lights and a television came out of the hideaway that was at the foot of his bed. He turned it on.

He put the volume low, and asked her if it bothered her. She said no and they lay there watching a movie. He stayed on his side and she on hers, but after a few moments, they ended up close to each other. She dozed off to sleep and felt him put his arm around her.

She awoke to the aroma of food cooking. When she went to use the bathroom, she was happy to see Colby had left a toothbrush and fresh towels. She showered and put on the robe that hung on the door, hoping it was okay. Then she made her way to the kitchen.

"I hope you don't mind," she said, indicating his robe.

"No, I don't mind. You look better in it than I do," he joked.

"Thank you," she said and took a seat.

"Question," he said seriously.

"Yes," she said wondering what was on his mind.

"Now this morning when I got up, I rubbed your hair away from your face and then I did a scalp check. No lie, be honest, is all that your real hair?"

She burst into laughter. "Yes, why?"

"No disrespect, I've never met one sister out here in L.A. who doesn't have a weave or extensions."

"Really?" she asked in disbelief.

"Yes, really. Not one. You are the very first."

"Wow, that's hard to believe, but hey, I've never thought about it. I guess that is rare out here."

Colby finished cooking and fixed their plates. He joined her at the table and they ate; then he took her home. He didn't leave until she agreed to go out with him later. She gave him a quick kiss and closed her door behind him.

She didn't want to get ahead of herself with thoughts of romance, but Colby was a happy start. She hung around the house, did a little cleaning, and watered her plants. She sat out on her patio, something she hadn't done in a while, and thanked God for what she had. She didn't have a huge and expensive mansion like Colby or Kory, but her place was spacious and modern with top-of-the-line everything and she could afford a decorator when she was stumped for ideas.

The show had done her well and she had a few dollars stacked. Not millions, but she wouldn't have to worry about going broke. Her house was paid for, so was her Beemer, and she didn't have a bunch of credit card debt. Working at the show had its perks, like free cosmetics, clothes, and so many other things that companies gave just to advertise on the show. Even her iPad had been free. She was going to miss it all, and prayed she'd land another gig soon.

She checked the time and saw it was close to five. Colby was going to pick her up by six thirty. She went to shower again and Rosalie, one of the makeup and hair stylists from the show, arrived on time to get her prettied up for her date.

She and Rosalie talked and she spilled the beans. When she told her who she had a date with, Rosalie squealed and almost dropped the curling iron. She had to force her to go when they were done, because she wanted to stick around and meet Colby. Wanting to impress him, Tiffany didn't want him to know her hair and makeup were done by a professional. She gave Rosalie her normal $200 fee and got her out just in time to slip on her dress, put on her jewelry, and hit the right spots with her Flower Bomb.

She was ready when he arrived at six thirty on the dot.

on't
and t
ted ar
t's like
that ne
ready for it to be gone yet.
hang out, and enjoy each
ke we've been doing, and
ur relationship to that level,
ch other enough to still miss
ve're apart."

but then again, it didn't make
dn't had any in a while and she
ease, but he was playing games.
lass of pinot and a foot massage
me," she said.

gave her a quick peck, and went
en to fix them both a drink. "Can
ke this upstairs?" she asked when
. "That chair in your room feels like
my grandma's arms."

problem," he said.

, she took off her clothes and took the
row from the ottoman and wrapped it
er body. She relaxed in the chair and
the ottoman in front of her and began
sage her feet. She closed her eyes and
his strong hands and that comfortable

Chapter Seventeen

Tiffany sat at her desk at work daydreaming about Colby. He was such a romantic, and she didn't know how much longer she could fight the feeling. She wanted to spread her legs wide open for him and she wanted to do it bad. They had been out countless times in a three-week period and she was on cloud nine whenever he was around. Since he hadn't tried to hit it, she had thought he might be gay, but he passed the gay test that Darryl put him to. She was elated he got the heterosexual seal of approval.

She wondered how to approach him. Should she show up in a trench naked or should she talk to him about it first? Either way, she wanted him.

Her intercom buzzed. "Tiffany, you have a call on line one," Myah said. "It's a Heather Tyson from TiMax."

Tiffany took the call quickly. "Hi, this is Tiffany Richardson."

"Hi, Miss Richardson, this is Heather Tyson. I am calling on behalf of Langley Green. He's wanted to speak with you for a while now. He'd like to meet you soon for lunch to discuss your show, *Boy Crazy*."

Tiffany almost dropped her phone. She remembered talking to Mr. Green about *Boy Crazy*, but she thought he had been blowing smoke up her ass. "Okay, I'd love to meet him to discuss it," she said, trying to sound calm.

"How is Thursday at one? I can call your assistant back with the details, if you'd like."

"Please do, and thank you, Miss Tyson." When she hung up, she screamed.

Myah ran through the door. "They want the show, don't they?" Tiffany could see she was trying to remain calm.

"I hope so, Mee-Mee. This could be it. He wants to meet with me on Thursday." She got up and hugged Myah, jumping up and down. "Heather is going to call you back with the details, Myah, so please make sure you get everything down."

"I will, I will, no doubt."

"This could be huge. If they sign the show, we will go global. This could be huge for *Boy Crazy*." Tiffany fell back into her chair. "I need a drink," she said, fanning herself with her hand. "Listen,

"Of course I do. I just
it. We are having a ball
what's keeping me exc
you every single day.
that anticipation and
be gone and I'm not
Let's just have fun,
other's company li
when we do take o
we'll care about ea
each other when
It made sense,
sense. Tiffany ha
was ready to rel
"Okay, Colby, a
sounds good to
He smiled,
into the kitch
we at least ta
he came bac
a big hug in
"Sure, no
Upstair
Chanel th
around h
he sat o
to mass
enjoye

chair. She sipped on her wine and gave him an occasional seductive look and he smiled. Once she finished her drink she was even hotter, but making a move on him would have been pointless. She climbed into his bed and did what she normally did in his bed: fell right to sleep.

A couple days later, she was ready for her pitch. She had on her "I mean business" suit and walked into the restaurant to meet Mr. Green with confidence. She was going to sell everything but her soul to get a contract with TiMax and seal this deal. She was going to listen, and if she had to make some changes to her ideas, she was prepared to compromise.

"Mr. Green," she said when she reached their table.

He stood. "Miss Richardson, so glad that you could make it." They shook hands and took their seats.

"I wouldn't have missed this meeting for the world."

A server came over to take their drink order. She ordered a soda.

Mr. Green shook his head. "Bring me a Scotch on the rocks, and the young lady will have an apple martini. You look like a martini girl," he said to Tiffany. She smiled and nodded. "Listen, Tiffany," he said when the server left, "I am not all business. We are people, not machines, so we are going to chat and discuss the show, so loosen up. If it takes a couple martinis to get you loose, we can drink before business. I want you to give me the true you, not what you think I want to hear you. I love your show. I've watched the last three weeks of it and I brought you here to make an offer. I am willing to hear your plans and the direction you want to go with the show, but I came here to make a deal."

Before she could reply, the server was back with their drinks. She realized the rich didn't have the long wait time that ordinary people had.

"Well, Mr. Green, I wanted to tell you the direction I'd like to take the show in and how long it lasts is how long it may last," she said nervously. "I want the girls to start the new season graduating from college. I want them to start their adventure in life learning things kind of the hard way. You know, broken hearts, trouble finding work, maybe issues with sexual harassment, dating a guy with a little penis," she added.

"Or a guy with an enormous one," Mr. Green joked.

Tiffany could see he was in tune with where she was going. "Exactly. Just things that young women experience. Then we move over to engagements a couple seasons in, maybe a pregnancy scare, just something to keep the humor and give relatable shows with realistic scenarios."

After bouncing several show ideas off one another, they were finished with their drinks and he signaled for the server to get them another. They threw in a quick lunch order and then it was back to business.

"What about nudity and profanity?" he asked. "TiMax is an adult channel and our series are for an adult audience."

"Well, the three main characters are on board for whatever changes that may come. My writers are talented and grown, and we are not afraid of nudity or profanity. It's hard for us to write without it," she joked. He laughed with her.

"Good, good," he said and took a drink. "Tiffany, I am going to be honest. I've already decided to sign the show. What happens now is the offer. Now, for the first two seasons, things will be standard. The only way the next season will change is if you get in there and rock the network."

Tiffany thought she'd burst.

"Now," he continued, "I want everyone who has been on to stay on. As far as the cast, as long as the three main characters sign, we have a show. As far as casting, writing, producing, and all that jazz, it is on you."

Their food came and Mr. Green conveniently changed the subject. After their meal, when the table was cleared, he went straight back to it. He reached into his briefcase and gave her offer letters for the cast members and general offer letters for her writers. They were standard and the numbers looked good. Way more than KCLN.

"Sir, I have one more question. My personal assistant, I really want to bring her with me. She is only making thirty-eight grand a year at KCLN, but she has benefits for her children."

"Okay, well, if she is your personal assistant, we'll give her forty-five grand and benefits." His words were music to Tiffany's ears. "I'll have her offer typed up and sent to you and I will give you until Monday to get back to me with the signed contracts. From there, we decide whether we will premiere next spring or fall."

Tiffany couldn't wait to meet with her people. They were as good as signed. She knew no one was going to walk away from this contract. How could they? It was more money and a larger audience.

When the meeting was done, Mr. Green stood to shake her hand. "I admire your drive, young lady. You are doing well for yourself and I know your father must be proud."

"Well, I never knew my father," she confessed. "My brother and I were raised by my mom. We struggled, but I am who I am today because of her hard work and sacrifice."

"I'm sorry, young lady. Your dad has no idea how blessed he is to have a daughter like you," he said and smiled.

Tiffany's eyes watered. She wished she had a dad to make proud, but she didn't. "Thank you, sir. And thank you so much for this opportunity. You won't regret it."

"I know I won't. Have a good day, Tiffany, and I look forward to seeing you soon." He shook her hand again and they parted.

She went back to her office glowing. She stopped at Myah's desk first and told her to come into her office. Myah handed her an envelope.

"What's this?"

"I don't know; it came by messenger a minute ago." She followed Tiffany into her office.

Tiffany set her briefcase down and ripped opened the envelope. It held two tickets to a play that was in town. It had a note attached:

Thanks for meeting with me today.
Please enjoy the show.

It was signed by Mr. Green. Pleased, she stuffed them back into the envelope. She would take Colby.

Now she got down to business. She told Myah the good news first and Myah was ready to do cartwheels. She told her to get a hold of the cast members to set up a meeting, and to tell her writers to meet her in the idea room.

When they gathered, she brought them up to speed and handed out the contracts. As she expected, everyone signed but Brad. He declined the offer. Tiffany didn't even ask why. She had already heard through the grapevine that he was going to sign with another show as executive producer.

Later, the cast assembled and she gave them the news. They were as happy as everyone else. She had all contracts signed but Brad's, but she didn't shed a tear about him. They could continue without him.

She didn't have to wait until Monday to call Mr. Green back, but she did. She spent the weekend lusting after Colby and decided she'd take a little break from him. The following weekend after her meeting with Mr. Green, her show had a home with TiMax. She celebrated with her cast and crew and didn't invite Colby.

The Friday before she headed to KCLN, she got a package from him. She opened it and found lingerie and instructions. Pulling back must have worked, because now it seemed as if he was sexually interested.

She couldn't wait for their weekend to begin.

Chapter Eighteen

The car pulled up to pick Tiffany up at her house. She had her overnight bag, and carried the exotic outfit and stilettos that Colby sent her in the original gift bag they came in. The driver got out, grabbed her bags, and put them into the trunk. He opened the door and she got in.

They drove away and she wondered where they were going, because he wasn't driving toward Colby's place. They finally stopped in front of Evolve, a pole dancing studio. She wondered why they were there. The driver got out, came around, and opened her door.

"Wh . . . wh . . . what are we doing here?" she asked, not moving to get out of the limo.

"I was told to bring you here, ma'am," he said.

She looked at him like he was crazy. "For what?" she asked.

A woman came out and approached the limo. "I'll take it from here, James," she said to the driver. He stepped aside. "Hi, Tiffany, my name is Marvelous. The studio has been reserved for you to learn a routine for your performance tonight."

Tiffany was even more confused. "Performance? What? What's going on?"

"Get out of the car, Tiffany, and come inside so I can fill you in."

She got out and walked slowly, still wondering what the hell was going on.

"Colby decided he'd give you a gift that you can give to him," Marvelous said, "so you are here to learn a pole dancing routine that is going to make the first encounter with your hot, sexy-ass boyfriend a night he will never forget. The outfit that he sent you is what you're going to wear tonight to do your bad-ass routine. I'm going to teach you a sexy-ass routine and the rest will be up to you, Cherry."

"It's Tiffany," she corrected her, wondering who could confuse the name Tiffany with a piece of fruit.

They walked into the studio. "It's Cherry in these walls, darling. We only have sexy names within these walls, and Tiffany is not sexy, honey."

"I can't learn a routine in this," she said, pointing to her clothes.

"We have that covered. Step right into this dressing room and change into the items on the seat."

Tiffany did as she instructed. When she came out, Marvelous was ready to get started.

"So, tell me what your daily routine is," the instructor said. "Do you exercise at all?"

"No," Tiffany said, wondering why that mattered. She was happy with her curves, and as long as her ass was bigger than her gut, she was satisfied with herself.

"That means your muscles are not loose, so we are going to do some warming up before we start to loosen them up. After that, we will start with the basics and then I'm going to teach you a killer routine."

They got started. Three hours later, she had her routine down, but she was exhausted. She showered and changed back into her clothes. The car was waiting outside for her and when she got in, there was a gift on the seat. She opened it and read the card:

Enjoy your spa treatments and massage.

The driver took her to the Ritz-Carlton. She got a massage, mani, pedi, brow and bikini wax, and had her hair and makeup done after she took another shower.

She was ready for the night to begin. She was starving. Her entire day had been spent preparing for Colby, but there were no meals in between.

The driver took her to a club. There were no cars in the lot. James opened her door and took her bags from the trunk. He escorted her in and she found Marvelous waiting. The woman took her to the back to change and told her that Colby was the only one in the audience waiting for her. She was instructed to go out there as Cherry, not Tiffany.

Tiffany nodded. She was nervous, but she was ready to turn her man on. The music started and that was her cue. She stepped out onto the stage. Colby was front and center. She tried to remember the routine that she learned earlier, but she had to add her own moves to keep from stopping when she forgot. By the end of her routine, the stage floor was full of bills. He had definitely made it rain. Tiffany wondered if he was really tipping her or if he wanted his money back. She went to the edge of the stage and kissed him.

"Was that hot enough for you?"

"Baby, you have no idea," he said and kissed her again. "Go and get changed and I'm going to take you to dinner and then we are going to go and handle some things."

She rushed to get dressed. They went to the restaurant, but Tiffany no longer had an appetite for food. She was in a romantic mood and was ready to feed her sexual appetite. She couldn't help but stare at Colby. He was a little less than six feet tall and had skin like a Hershey bar. It was smooth and blemish free. If he weren't an actor, he could have easily been a model, even an underwear model because he had a killer body. Since she now had a new home for *Boy Crazy*, she was definitely going to ask him to consider being a guest star or even a permanent role.

She took a few sips of her wine and was anxious for the food to come so they could get back to his place.

"So how'd you like the show?" she asked him.

"I loved the show. You were hot, baby," he said and took a drink.

"Oooh, hot. I like that description."

Finally, their food came. They did very little eating, but a whole lot of flirting. After dinner, they sat and finished their drinks. Colby's phone rang.

"Hold on, babe, it's my agent." He stood and stepped away from the table. When he returned, he had a look of disappointment on his face.

"Colby, what's wrong?" she asked.

"Well, Rick just called and said that I am up for an audition for a Bill Connelly film."

She wondered why he was so sad about that. "Colby, that's awesome, babe. Why the long face?"

"If I want the opportunity, I have to catch a flight to New York tonight."

Her smile faded. "Tonight? Please not tonight."

"I'm sorry, Tiffany, but you know how it goes. Opportunity only knocks once for roles like this."

She knew he was right, but didn't feel any better about it. "I know, Colby," she whined. "But tonight was supposed to be our night."

"I know, and I will make it up to you. I promise."

They left in a hurry. Colby had to get home and pack a bag and get to the airport. She went with him and watched him pack a small bag and then she rode with him to the airport. She kissed him bye and the driver took her home. She rode in the back of the limo horny and angry. She didn't even know how long he would be gone.

She tried to suck it up and let it go, but her hormones were on ten and she needed to release an orgasm before she exploded. "Why tonight of all nights?" she asked herself. It felt like they were never going to have sex.

When she got home, she washed the layers of makeup from her face, ran a bubble bath, and hit the button on her iPod dock. She scrolled to Fantasia again and put it on random. She went into the kitchen and poured herself a glass of Chardonnay and went back to step into her tub. She tried calling Colby, but it went straight to voice mail and she figured his flight had taken off. She soaked and sipped, and after the water was cool, she lathered, rinsed, and got out. She tried to keep her eyes open and wait for him to call, but she lost that battle.

The next morning, she was surprised he hadn't called when he landed.

"Okay, Tressa, I did what you asked. I made sure she'd leave Kory alone, but now she is ready to be intimate and I don't know how long I can keep her off. I mean, she is really starting to catch feelings for me. I thought I could handle this, but I'm not attracted to her like that. She is cool and all and spending time with her is great, but if I have sex with her, not being egotistical or anything, but she is going to be on me like white on rice, and I don't want to hurt her."

Tressa sighed. "Colby, when I came to you to help me out on this, I thought you knew sex came with the territory. Not only am I paying you well, I am going to make sure you get a hit series on TiMax. But you gotta keep Tiffany away from my man until we are married. Once I am married, I'll get my trust and a spot at TiMax. Until I'm married, my dad isn't going to budge."

"Tressa, until you're married was not the agreement. You said you wanted me to take her out, spend some time with her to get Kory off her mind and her off his and then that's it. You're certainly not paying me well enough to sleep with her," he disputed looking down at his phone. It was Tiffany, so he hit IGNORE. He was supposed to be on a plane to New York. This fake trip would only buy him a week away from her tops. He knew when he saw her again she was going to be ready for some action.

"Are you kidding me, Colby? I'm paying for everything as it is. On top of your high-ass fee. I don't have my trust fund yet and I'm going broke with you romancing the hell out of her."

"All this extra shit was your idea, Tressa, because you wanted her out of Kory's face. I'm just doing what you hired me to do, and that was to take her attention off your fiancé." He reached into his bag, pulled out the video camera, and handed it to her. "Here. I have no idea what you plan to do with a pole dancing recording, but here you go."

"Oh, don't worry about this video, Colby. This is just ammo. What you need to worry about is how you are going to keep Miss Tiffany occupied until I jump the broom. After I get my money and get your hit show going, Kory can leave if he wants and be with her. Our show is going to make *Boy Crazy* look like last season's fashion, and my dad is going to recognize me for my talents. So name your price. How much will it take for you to consummate this relationship? Because I am not going to lose my trust fund or my man. Kory is the first man my daddy has given his blessing to for my hand in marriage, and if he calls this wedding off I'll be at square one. I'm almost thirty-two. I need my trust!"

He knew she was serious, but there wasn't a dollar amount to make him want to sleep with Tiffany. He was already ashamed of what he was doing to her without the sex. "Tressa, I don't want more money. I just want to break up with her already and not go there with her sexually."

"So you like her too?"

"What?"

"You like her, Colby." She moved to the bar to fix a drink. "You were all for hooking up with her and doing what I asked. You were like, 'It's just acting,' and now you are ready to quit on me? What makes this big-boned heifer so irresistible? Really, she is not all that. I mean, tell me, what is the deal with this Tiffany Richardson?"

Colby decided to stick to his story. He liked her yes, Tiffany was hard to resist, but he didn't want to mix his business with pleasure. He went into this as only playing the role of Tiffany's boyfriend, and he didn't want to alter the script by catching feelings for her. That was another reason sex was not on his priority list. It was bad enough he was pretending to like her. Sleeping with her with no feelings for her was too much for him. He wanted his own hit series, yes, but it wasn't worth doing Tiffany in. If he got involved and she discovered what he did, she'd never speak to him again.

"Look, Tressa," he said. "I do not like her, okay? And for your information, Tiffany happens to be a great person. She is smart, ambitious, and her being big-boned is a plus in my book."

"All I need to know is that you're on board. All you have to do is keep her entertained and away from Kory. And if that means fucking her, Colby, make it happen. Get drunk, get high, and just get it in so she can get over my man. I will double your fee if I have to, just don't bail. If I don't marry Kory, I get nothing. I can't go back to square one. My dad is on the verge of cutting me off. I cannot go from riches to rags." She got in his face. "If I do, you will never land a role again. So do what needs to be done."

"Tressa, don't threaten me, okay? I'm helping your ass out. You are the one with the changes in the plan. A few dates and to run interference was the offer you put on the table for the fee you set up, along with a starring role on a TiMax series. I'm not a man whore and sleeping with Tiffany is just not going to happen." He got up to leave.

"Okay, listen, I hear you and I understand this moral code you got going on, but please, I'm begging you, Colby, keep her interested. My wedding is a handful of months away, and I need Tiffany to be a distant memory."

Colby could see the desperation in her eyes. "This is about the money, nothing more. I care about Kory, I do, but I want what's been promised to me since I was twenty-one years old. I've been in and out of rehab to please my father and Kory is my ticket. Once I get my money, he can run off with Tiffany if he wants."

"I will continue to see her, Tressa, but if she and I become physical, that's when the deal will be off. If I feel like sharing a bed with Tiffany, that will be because that's what I want, not because you're paying me. But you will get me my series."

"Done," she said.

He left, hating what he had done. He didn't mean to fall for Tiffany. He didn't know she'd be that great. Tressa had painted an opposite image of who Tiffany really was and he had thought she was a man-stealing bitch. After spending time with her and talking to her, he realized she wasn't the typical L.A. girl. She wasn't afraid to eat in public and she didn't mind throwing on a pair of tennis shoes and jeans. She was an intelligent, down-to-earth diva. She was sexy when she had to be, and loved sports. *Why, oh why, did I agree to this?* he asked himself as his limo pulled out of Tressa's driveway. He should have backed out after the third date, because by then, he wanted to see Tiffany again and again whether Tressa paid him or not.

When he got home, he decided he'd wait until morning to call Tiffany. He figured he'd tell her that he'd be home right after his alleged audition. He knew she'd want to see him and he knew she'd want to do what grown-ups do.

He made up his mind to go with the flow. If he was feeling it, he'd give her what she wanted.

Chapter Nineteen

The next morning Tiffany decided she'd go in to clean out her office. There were no more meetings or show talk, so it wasn't necessary for her to be at KCLN anymore. She was thrilled about her position at TiMax and Mr. Green had invited her to move in right away. She had only seen her new office once and hadn't moved anything into it yet. TiMax was excited about the show. They wanted to get the ball rolling immediately and get the show on their new fall lineup. She and her team were ready to work. She only had a couple weeks to be off and then they were back to creating episodes. She needed to meet with everyone to start on set ideas and other details for the show and she was anxious to get started.

After she took down her fourth box, she decided to drive over to TiMax to put some things into her office. She didn't want to leave them in the car and it didn't make sense to take them home and have to lug them inside and then back out to her car later. She pulled into the station and asked the guard at the sign-in gate for some quick directions. She found a close parking space, grabbed one box, and went inside. The building was quiet and she figured that was the norm for a Sunday.

She found her way to her new office and stood admiring the space. It was huge. Her old office didn't have shit on her new one. She looked out the window at the studio and different trailers and smiled. The entire lot was five times bigger than KCLN. She couldn't wait to get acquainted with everyone here.

She ran down to get another box and then made two more trips to get the other two. Since Colby was gone and she didn't have much going on that day, she decided she'd stick around and unpack. She opened the mini fridge and was floored. It was already stocked with soda and juice. She opened the cabinet that sat over it and found Belvedere, her favorite vodka. It was hanging out with a bottle of Cîroc, Grey Goose, Johnny Walker Black, Hennessy, and a couple of tropical rums.

"Sweet Jesus, I am going to love it here," she said. She moved over to the other cabinet and opened it. "Oh my God, there's more," she said when she saw the bottles of wine and champagne. The next cabinet held unopened juices and the final cabinet contained glasses. She turned the handle on the faucet and saw that the water really worked. She grabbed the ice bucket from the granite countertop and headed out to find the ice machine.

She followed the signs to the kitchen area. It looked like a kitchen in a home instead of one in an office building. There was a stove, a huge subzero fridge, and an overhead microwave. When she went around the counter and saw a dishwasher, she thought she was in work heaven. KCLN didn't have anything close to this. She opened the fridge. It was fully stocked with muffins, bagels, and yogurt. And nothing had a name on it. She pressed the ice button, but nothing came out. She opened the freezer. The ice container was empty and the lever was switched to off and she wondered why. She closed the freezer door and then felt foolish. Right next to the fridge was a huge ice machine, like the ones in a hotel. She filled her bucket and headed back to her office. On the way, she ran into Tressa and Wallace.

"Tressa," she said.

"Tiffany, what are you doing here?"

"I brought some things over to set up my office."

The shocked look on Tressa's face said she had no idea Tiffany worked there now. She blinked like she had something in her eyes. "Your office? Come again?"

"Yes, my office. Your dad didn't tell you? *Boy Crazy* has a home here at TiMax now. You didn't know?"

"No, I didn't. Did you, Wallace?" She looked at her companion.

"No, no one told me anything." He sounded just as surprised as Tressa.

"Well, I met your father at your engagement party. The funny thing is he had no idea who I was."

Tressa looked at Wallace again. "Wallace, you didn't tell Daddy about your meeting with Tiffany?"

"Well, ummm, ummm, your dad was out of town when I met with Tiffany and when I ran the idea by Mike," he said. Mike was Mr. Green's partner. "He's the one that gave it a no."

"Well I had no idea, Tiffany. I specifically remember telling Wallace to let my dad know that you were an old friend of Kory's. I am so sorry."

"It's all good, no harm done, love. I'm here now, right?" She headed back to her office. "Oh, and tell Kory I said hello," she said over her shoulder.

Tressa was hotter than a jalapeño pepper. She'd had no clue that her dad had given *Boy Crazy* a slot. She glared at Wallace. "How did you not know about this?"

"I don't know," he said. "No one said anything. There was no e-mail, no memo, no nothing," he said.

"Well, you are going to have to keep an eye on her, Wallace. If you want to continue to work here when I take over this company, you're going to have to step it up." She stormed out.

Back in her office, Tiffany fixed herself a vodka and cranberry. She pulled out her iPod and went over to the fancy little mini system that was on the opposite wall of her liquor stash. She hit the power button and put her iPod on the dock and went to her favorite CD by Fantasia. She scrolled to "Free Yourself" and when the music started, she continued to get her office set up. She thought about Kory briefly then channeled her brain to Colby. She smiled. She finally may have landed a man, a relationship with someone who was sexy, smart, and rich. "If only I knew how the sex is," she said. She took a swallow of her drink and wondered if his dick was embarrassingly small or if he was a minute man.

She just wanted to figure out why he was not interested in unclogging her drain. She finished up and broke down the boxes and put them in the hall by her office door, praying the cleaning service would pick them up. She downed her last swallow and went to put the glass in the sink. She rinsed it and headed out. She wanted to see what else this beautiful studio had to offer, so she took her time going back to her car. She stopped on different floors and checked out the fitness center and the pool. The theater was huge, much larger than the one at KCLN. She was proud of herself. She had come from the bottom to the top in less than four years. She had taken the chance that God gave her and done well. She was anxious to get in there and produce some new great shows.

When she finally made it to her car, her phone rang. It was Colby.

"Hey, you," she said with the widest smile on her face.

"Hey, where are you? I am at your place." he said.

"At my place? I thought you were in New York."

"I was, but I took an early flight back and I'm here. I wanted to surprise you."

"Well, I'm surprised. What happened to the audition?"

"It wasn't for me, babe, so I didn't even go."

"Awww, that's too bad," she said.

"Naw, it's all good. Where are you?"

"I'm leaving TiMax." She waved to the guard as she pulled out of the gate. "I came by to bring some of my stuff. Babe, my office is fantastic. It is stocked with liquor."

He laughed. "That's the only fantastic thing about it?"

"Ummm, pretty much, yeah."

"Okaaaaay," Colby said.

"So what's up?" she asked. "Why are you at my place, and without calling?"

"As I said, I wanted to surprise you. Imagine how surprised I was to get here with all of these beautiful roses and my baby ain't even home."

"Roses?"

"Yes, roses."

"Well it's going to take me about forty-five minutes. Even though it's the weekend, traffic is not nice."

"You're closer to my place than yours; how about you head to my place and I'll meet you there?"

"That sounds great, but I look a mess, Colby. Hair pulled up, jeans, flip-flops, and a T-shirt." She didn't want to see him looking so awful.

"I bet you look perfect."

"How about no," she said and giggled.

"Look, you don't have to dress up. We can hang around the house, throw some meat on the grill, and play a little pool. And after we watch a little TV, I can watch you bathe."

Tiffany's pussy contracted and she swerved. "Come again? Repeat that last part," she said.

"You heard me, watch you bathe. Your man can't take it anymore."

"Making a U-turn now. Will see you at your place." She pulled off the road to turn around.

They laughed and talked and when she made it to his house, he told her the hiding place for his spare key and the alarm code. "Are you sure you want to divulge the alarm code? I mean, I can wait in my car," she said.

"I trust you won't snoop."

He was right, but she messed with him. "How can you be so sure? I mean, I am a woman and we snoop."

"Well, so far, you are the most unusual woman I've ever dated. I've never dated a woman who was drama-free and without hair extensions."

"With that said, I won't snoop. I'll fix a drink and go out to the patio and wait for you."

"Okay, I will see you soon. I am just going to run by the grocery store, pick up a couple steaks to grill, and I'll be there.

"Okay, Colby, I'll see you soon," she said and ended the call.

She did exactly what she said she would do: fixed a vodka and cranberry and went out and watched the pool water dance in the gentle breeze. When Colby got home, he came out and greeted her with a warm smile.

She stood and put her arms around his neck and gave him a kiss, thinking she was now the queen of L.A.

Chapter Twenty

"Daddy!" Tressa yelled when she walked into the house. "Dad!" she yelled again when there was no answer.

Tina, one of their staff members, informed her that he was in his study. Tressa rushed over and burst through the door.

"Isabella," he said, looking up with a frown.

"Daddy, what's going on?"

"What do you mean? And why did you come through the door like that?"

"*Boy Crazy,* Daddy. How could you sign that show when I asked you not to? I told you Tiffany is Kory's ex-lover and I don't want any dealings with her."

"Isabella, as I told you, you don't have to have any dealings with Miss Richardson. She works for me, not you, and your personal feelings have absolutely nothing to do with my business."

"But, Daddy, when I take over the com . . . I mean, come aboard, I am going to have to deal with her."

He laughed. "Isabella, you have a lot to prove before you ever take over, and a lot of work to do before you even hold a seat on the board. You need to focus on your wedding and getting married and starting a life with Kory, clean and sober. Your past isn't far behind you, and I don't know when I'll be giving you a seat on the company's throne. You have to show me that you are responsible and commit yourself to something other than shopping and partying."

"Daddy, how can you say that? You told me once I'm married and doing well, you would bring me on."

"Yes, once you are married and can show me that you're ready to work and be a part of TiMax."

"But, Daddy," she whined, "I am."

"No, Isabella, you're not. You'd be willing to let a hit show walk because of some high school romance. Kory is marrying you, princess, and that should be enough to set aside your childish notions of 'Tiffany trying to take yo' man,'" he said, imitating her. "I gave *Boy Crazy* a contract because it is a hit show. Tiffany works hard and deserves to keep the show going on her merit, so grow up and act like a woman, Tressa. There are only a handful of black shows on television and I have the power to keep a great one going, but because of your personal insecurities, you don't want to see it go on. You're not a little girl anymore, Isabella. You can't come into my office whining and throwing tantrums to get your way, especially when it comes to my network. This is what TiMax needs, a hit series.

"You are always so busy thinking of yourself and that is why I have withheld your trust four times. You are not ready, Isa, your mind is not business-oriented yet, and I don't know why. You have to give me something, Isabella, to show me that I can trust you with a chair at my network or even with your trust. You are going to make me change your trust again if you don't grow up," he threatened and stood up.

"*Por favor, no papá,*" she said, with tears and in Spanish, the only language they used around her mother. She knew she wasn't responsible or the business-headed daughter he dreamed of having, but she wanted her money and wanted to have some control at the network.

"*Ya g. No eres una niña pequeña.*" He left the room.

Tressa went looking for her momma to talk some sense into her daddy. But when she found her, her mom said the same thing, she needed to grow up. She was not a baby anymore. She left frustrated and was about to head to Kory's, but

Stephen called and she needed what he had for a quick pick-me-up.

She drove with the wheels turning in her head, thinking of all the things she could do to shut Tiffany and her show down. Business or not, she wanted that bitch to move back to Chicago until she was married. Even though Kory denied it, she knew he slept with Tiffany the night of their engagement party. He had never turned her down for sex, and for him to come home and want to shower and go to sleep was a dead giveaway. She didn't want them to be within fifteen feet of each other or even share the same air space again. She hoped Colby would lay it on her to keep her away from Kory.

She pulled up in front of Stephen's place and found a party going on. She called Kory and told him not to wait up. When he began to drill her, she wanted to hang up in his face, but she promised him she'd come over right after. She went inside and joined her party friends, heading straight for the coke. After she took her second line, she went for the bubbly. She knew she was supposed to be clean and sober, but she was under a lot of pressure with the wedding, paying Colby a grip to entertain Tiffany, and now she had to deal with the fact that her father gave that trick a spot for her show. She just wanted to forget about all the bullshit that was going on and coke gave her that release.

She left the party in a cab. When she got to Kory's, she leaned on the doorbell until he finally opened the door.

"Sweetie, the cabby is ninety dollars and I'm outta cash," she slurred and began to giggle.

He paid the driver and helped her inside. "You're drunk, Tressa!" he yelled. "Why are you drinking? You know you are not supposed to be drinking."

"Look, I'm not off the fuckin' wagon, okay?" She spoke with a drunken drawl. "I am under a lot of fuckin' stress planning our fuckin' fantastical, enormous, fantabulous wedding. And . . . and . . . and . . . and . . . tonight, I needed to get loose." She fell back onto the couch and within seconds, was passed out.

Kory tried to wake Tressa. "Reesy, come on, babe, let's go upstairs." He shook her again. "Reesy, baby, come on."

Her purse fell off of her lap and the contents fell out. He bent down to get them and saw a coke vial. He picked it up and sat beside her on the sofa in disbelief. Disappointed and hurt, all he could do was sob into his hands. He had trusted her, dealt with her lies, and ignored the truth.

Sighing, he put her purse on the couch beside her and went up to bed. It took him awhile, but eventually he fell asleep.

The next morning, he was up and she was still passed out. After four that afternoon he sat on the love seat and watched her sleep. When she woke, she saw him staring at her.

She sat up. "Damn, Kory, why are you sitting there staring at me? What time is it?"

"It's time for you to come clean and tell me the truth."

"Come on, Kory, it's too early for the third degree. My head is banging and I need some coffee," she said, standing and staggering to the bathroom.

He was waiting in the kitchen when she came out. "I'm going to ask you once, Reesy, and I want the truth."

"I will tell you whatever you want, just please don't talk to me until I've had a cup of coffee," she said starting the coffeemaker.

He watched her move around the kitchen in her expensive party dress and smeared makeup. She looked around and located a hair clamp and pulled her hair up. Her momma was Mexican and her dad was black, but she had her mom's hair texture. Even though it was long, she still wore extensions to make it fuller. After she poured herself a cup of coffee, she walked past Kory and sat on a stool at the island in the middle of the room.

He waited until after she finished drinking and asked, "Are you good now?"

"Yes, now where's the fire?" she snapped.

"Are you using again?"

Frowning, "Kory, what kinda question is that?"

"Are you using again?" he yelled.

"Look, I know I got drunk last night. I will be going back to AA, okay, but I'm not using." She looked away.

"Tressa, don't lie to me."

"Fuck, Kory, no, a'ight? I told you that I was done with that."

"Get your things, Tressa, the wedding is off."

She hopped up. "What? What's wrong with you?"

"You heard me. Oh, and here, don't forget to pack this." He put the vial on the island in front of her and walked away.

"Oh my God, Kory, that's not mine. Cee-Cee . . . that belongs to Cee-Cee," she cried.

"If that is Cee-Cee's, what was it doing in your damn purse?"

"What, you went through my shit?" she shouted.

"No," he yelled. "Your shit fell out of your purse when you passed out on the couch this morning. Now leave."

"Wait, Kory. Wait, sweetheart. Please wait a minute. Don't call the wedding off, Kory, please. Yes, last night I snorted a couple lines of coke, but it's not like before. I'm not on that shit like that anymore, I promise you. I was stressed out and I did a line or two. Stephen gave this to me. I had no intention of using it, I swear," she cried.

While he watched, she went over to the sink, turned on the water, and opened the vial. She emptied the contents down the drain, but he still didn't believe a word from her lying lips.

"Really, Tressa, really? I know you've been using. For a whole minute now, I've known. Like . . . like, as soon as we got engaged, you changed. I ignored it, but I can't anymore. I don't want to marry you and I want you to leave."

"Kory, listen, we can work this out, okay? I'll go back into rehab if that's what you want, just please don't call off the wedding. Please, I love you," she cried.

"No, Tressa, you love you. All you think of is what Tressa wants and what Tressa needs. And you know what, Tressa, I don't want to be with you anymore. I don't love you. I thought I did and tried to convince myself that I do, but I don't. Now I am willing to pay your father back for every dime he has spent. The wedding is off."

"Oh God, my dad. You can't tell him, Kory. Please, I'm begging you. If my dad finds out, he is going to disown me. I can't lose you and my family, Kory. Please don't tell him."

"Tressa, I . . . I won't tell him. I just want you to leave. We are done."

"I'll go, but promise, Kory, that you won't tell my dad."

"I won't; now get what you need, because I have somewhere to go."

"Tiffany, right?" she whispered and sniffled.

"Just get your things, Reesy." He went up to shower. He was going to Tiffany's, but that wasn't her business.

Chapter Twenty-one

"No, no, no," Tiffany cried at the sight of her menstrual. She knew it was coming in a couple days, but it was there now. Her plans to get down with Colby that night were a bust. She stood, washed her hands, and went back to the living room where he was waiting. "Colby, I have to go," she said sadly.

"Why? I thought tonight was going to be our night," he said.

"I know, but I have a visitor; she came unannounced."

He looked confused at first, then comprehension dawned. "Oooh, that visitor."

She nodded. "Yes, and I need to get home because I don't have anything on me."

He kissed her on the forehead. "It's cool, Tiff. Our time will come."

"Yeah, next year. I mean, damn, it's always something."

"I know, but at least this will be over in a few days. And then . . ." He smiled.

"Yeah, yeah. I must go. I will call you," she said and made her way to the door.

"Okay, drive safe and I'll see you soon." He gave her a final kiss.

The next day, Tiffany was in her comfortable pajamas on the sofa with her favorite blanket. She hated being on her menstrual because she still cramped so bad. She took a couple of pain pills then said the heck with the rules and poured herself a glass of wine. She popped in *Just Wright* to watch again and called Colby. She convinced him that she was in no mood for company, and he agreed to let her chill.

Around eight and halfway through the movie, the doorbell rang and she smiled. She knew Colby would come by anyway. She did a quick mirror check and went for the door. When she opened it, she was shocked to see that it was Kory.

"What are you doing here?" she asked, not inviting him in.

"Can I come in?" he asked.

She folded her arms. "Where is your fiancée?"

"Look, Tiff, the wedding is off and I really need to talk."

She stepped aside and let him in. "I'm sorry, Kory." She looked closely at him and noted he looked terrible. "Would you like something to drink?"

"A Scotch, rum, brandy on the rocks is fine. Whatever you have dark." He flopped down on the couch.

"Of course," she said and hurried to the kitchen. She poured him a drink and went back to the living room and handed it to him. He downed it and asked for a refill. "What happened?" she asked, sitting down across from him.

"Do you want me to start from the beginning or just at today?" He took a huge swallow of his drink.

"Start wherever you want to start. I'm here to listen." Her heart was racing. She had Colby, she told herself, so why was her heart doing flips and why was she excited that he and the queen of L.A. were done?

"You were right," he said.

"What was I right about?" she asked, confused. She'd never told him her thoughts about Tressa.

"Tressa is using again." She opened her mouth to deny it and he held up a hand to stop her. "I know it was you who told Keith, so don't deny it." He looked at his empty glass and his eyes welled.

She knew he needed another drink, so she stood and took his glass. When she came back to hand him his refill, he grabbed her, put his face to her stomach, and sobbed.

She rubbed his head. "Kory, shhh. Tressa just wasn't the right one."

"I know, Tiffany. I tried to be stand-up and stand by the commitment I made to her, but after seeing you again, things changed. I'm upset because I was asking God for a way out."

Her hand stilled. "Kory, this has nothing to do with us. Tressa needs help; she is an addict." Darryl had called her that morning and told her about the party, but she had vowed to stay out of it.

"I know that, Tiff, but I am relieved because I want to be with you."

She stepped away from him and dropped back onto the other sofa. "Kory, you are not thinking clearly. You were just engaged to Tressa."

"Yes, and that night I came here, the night of the engagement party, I wanted to be with you so bad, Tiff. You've been on my mind ever since."

She suddenly needed a fan. The love of her life was right in front of her face and she couldn't do shit. She was with Colby and on her cycle, so she had to use her brain and block out what her heart was screaming in Dolby

Surround sound. It yelled at her, saying, *Move over close to him and tell him you want him too*. But her brain reminded her about her sweet and fine-ass boyfriend, Colby.

"Listen, Kory," she said, "I'm sorry about Tressa and the way things turned out. A few weeks ago, I would have been doing back flips on my lawn with the news of your wedding being off, but I am involved. I'm seeing someone."

The color left his face. He got up and went into the kitchen. Her floor plan was open, so she saw him fix another drink for himself. He downed it and poured another before he returned and sat back down.

"Are you happy, Tiffany?" he asked, his voice shaking.

"Yes," she whispered. She looked at the muted television, unable to look at him.

"I need the bathroom," he said and stood up.

She pointed the way and sat nervously on the sofa, wondering what thoughts were going through his mind. When he finally returned, she didn't take her eyes off the television.

"Listen, I'm sorry I came here talking about us. I'm happy you've met someone." He paused. "I really need a moment, do you mind?"

When she shook her head, he sat back down on the sofa and lay back. Ten minutes later, he was snoring, so she got up and got him a blanket. She got back on the other sofa, pulled her blanket up, and restarted her movie. She turned the volume on low, and after a while she dozed off.

When she got up to go to the bathroom, he was still asleep. She went and did her business and then went back into the living room and shook him. "Kory," she said. He opened his eyes and looked up. "Why don't you come to the bed," she offered.

He declined and said he was going to head home, but she insisted because it was after one in the morning. He headed toward the guest room, but she remembered the bed was not made because she never put the sheets back on after she had washed them.

"No, this way," she said. He followed her into her room. "That bed is not made and I have a king size. I'm sure we can share a bed as friends, right?" He nodded.

She got on the opposite side of the bed from what she was used to sleeping on while he took off his shoes and lifted his shirt over his head. She looked at his jeans and knew it would be a mistake, but she wanted him to be comfortable.

"It's okay to take your jeans off. You do have on boxers underneath, right?"

He stopped as if thinking and then stood to pull them off. She got a peep at his dick when he climbed into the bed through the slit in the front of his boxers. Even though it wasn't erect, she imagined it could grow into a pleasurable size. She closed her eyes, lay back on her pillow, and told her inside voice to stop talking about Kory's dick.

"Thank you," he said.

"What for?" she asked, confused.

"For letting me stay. I honestly didn't want to go home alone tonight."

She looked over at him. "Anytime. I know if the tables were turned, you'd do the same for me."

He smiled a gorgeous smile. "Yes, I would. And, Tiff, I'm happy that you're happy." He closed his eyes.

"Thank you," she said and turned over to go to sleep. Not long after, he was holding her and it felt nice. She snuggled into him.

The next morning she got up to hurry to the bathroom. When she looked over, he had an erection. She covered her mouth, marveling at how huge it was. She wanted to see skin, so she gently pulled the little opening on his fly. The sight of the stiffness with veins popping out everywhere made her mouth water and her pussy clench. She quickly pulled away and rushed into the bathroom.

When she returned, the show was over; it had deflated. She climbed back into bed, and although she had a man, she took advantage of the one that was currently in her bed and cuddled up close to him.

Before she could fall back into a deep sleep, she felt his erection again. She pressed her ass up against him even closer.

Chapter Twenty-two

Tiffany was headed to Colby's when her cell phone chirped. It was Kory. She didn't want to reply, but she did, telling him she was headed to Colby's. He texted again and asked if she could stop by before going, he had something he needed to discuss.

She texted him back:

Can it wait til 2morrow?

His next text said it couldn't. She ignored it and kept driving in Colby's direction. She got another text:

Please. I won't keep you long.

She made a detour and headed for his house. She hit the speed dial button and called Colby.

"Hey, babe, I am going to be a little later than planned. Is that okay? I have to make a quick stop."

"How much later? These last five days not seeing you have been hell." The first couple of days, she had kept him away from her place for fear that Kory would drop by unannounced.

"I know, Colby, and I am dying to see you, but you know Kory just broke off his engagement and he is a mess."

"I know, but your man is dying to see you. How about you invite him over? Maybe if he hung out with us, we both could help him out. You know what, maybe we should hook him up. I have a friend who is a model and she is hot."

"Colby, he just broke up with his fiancée; he may not be interested in getting hooked up." She omitted the fact that she didn't want the love of her life being hooked up.

"How do you know that? The old saying is 'If you want to get over someone, find someone new to help you get over them.'" He quoted it all wrong, but she knew what he meant.

"Listen, I am just going to run by and check on him and then I'm all yours."

"Okay, if you must, you must. Just don't keep me waiting long. I'm ready to hear you moan."

"I won't be long, I promise," she said and ended the call.

Traffic was horrible, so it took her longer to get to Kory's than she anticipated. When she got to the door, he opened the door looking sexier than ever. She wanted to run back to her car. She liked Colby, but there was still a place in her heart for Kory.

"Hey, Tiff, hey," he said and let her in. "Thank you so much for coming."

"I would have been here sooner, but traffic was a monster." She followed him in and laid her purse on the sofa. "So what's up, what did you want to talk about?"

"Would you like something to drink?" he asked.

"Sure," she said. "Just a quick one."

He dashed off to the kitchen and came back with a glass of Merlot. "I hope red is okay."

She took the glass from his extended hand and took a sip. "Red is fine, Kory. What's up, why did you want me to come over?"

"How about we go outside," he suggested. They went out the French doors to his outdoor living space and got comfortable on the couches.

"Kory, I can't stay long. I'm meeting Colby soon." She looked at her watch.

"That's what I wanted to talk about. I, ummm, talked with Amber, Reesy's friend, earlier today and she told me some things about Tressa that I didn't know. And she also told me something about Colby." Kory thought back to his conversation with the wedding planner. He had called her to ask her about any outstanding balance that was left from the cancelled wedding so he could take care of it and she agreed to meet with him. After they had gone over the wedding business, she remembered he called her a couple weeks back, but she never returned his call.

"Look, I'm sorry I didn't get back to you when you call me the other week. Being pregnant and a doctor's wife is full-time work, and I honestly forgot to give you a call back."

"It's cool. I know the answer to the question I had, but there are still a few things running around my mind that I'd like you to help me with."

"What do you wanna know?" she asked.

"Everything," he said.

"Okay, ask what you wanna ask. If I know, I will tell you."

"I know Tressa is on drugs, but was she having an affair?" he asked first. She laughed. "What's funny?"

"Tressa wasn't having an affair, Kory; at least I don't know of any. Sex is at the bottom of her to-do list. She is messed up when it comes to intimacy. She has been in some physical situations before you, and that has her messed up in the head when it comes to sex. I'm only telling you this because I know she has issues and needs help. But no matter how I've tried to help her, she refuses to get it. Truth is . . ." She leaned in close. "Can I say the truth?" she asked. Kory nodded. "She gave you horrible head jobs just so you wouldn't ask her for it."

He was speechless at first. Then he shook his head. "That comes as no surprise. I know she couldn't have been just that horrible at it." They both laughed a little.

"Yes, and as much as I used to dread it, my man loves it, so I had to perfect it," she said, rubbing her belly and giggling a little.

"Okay, tell me, why did Tressa want to marry me? I mean, she is worth four times more than me. My family has the jewelry business and whatnot, but Mr. Green has billions and she can get any actor, celeb, or athlete she wants."

"For the money," Amber said.

"Money? You are mistaken. Tressa is loaded. She doesn't need my money."

"Not your money, her trust fund. Her dad has changed the terms a billion times because she has not proven responsible enough to have it. Now, at thirty-one, her dad said he won't give it to her until she marries an honest man for love and makes it for at least a year. You are an

*honest man, not Hollywood or an athlete, and
as long as you love her and marry her, after a
year, she will get her trust. I don't know if she
loves you. All I know is if this marriage would
have taken place and y'all made it at least
one year, she would have inherited over forty
million dollars. Her own money. No more per-
mission from her daddy, but her own money.
No more depending on Mommy and Daddy to
pay this or that. No more spending limits and
so forth, and she wouldn't have to go to them
for anything.*

  *"She is a rich girl, but most of the things she has
is because her mother goes behind Mr. Green's
back to do extra. But she is on a budget and her
taste exceeds her budget. I mean, she gets a few
gigs here and there on shows and make appearances, has her own cosmetic and fragrance lines,
but her daddy's pocket is where the real money is.
You're the first man Mr. Green has approved of
and adored, so that is why she wanted to marry
you."*

  *Kory felt horrible for being played by her. He
forced a smile. "Listen, Amber, thank you for
giving me some closure." He stood to leave.*

  "Wait, there is one other thing," she said.

  He sat back down. "What?"

"It's about your friend, Tiffany."

Now he was sitting next to Tiffany, ready to disclose the horrible news he had received.

"Okay then, let's hear it," she said. She took a sip of wine and looked at him.

"Colby is a fraud."

"Excuse me?" she asked, leaning in.

"Colby is not who he says he is."

"Colby is Colby," she said laughing. She took another sip. "What are you talking about, Kory? You're not making any sense."

"Tiff, how long have you known this cat? I mean, seriously, do you think he is stand-up?"

"Kory, you are shitting me right?" she snapped. "You ask me to come over to put some bullshit in my ear about Colby not being the one?"

"Look, Tiff, all I'm saying is you should be careful, you know. Take it slow. This guy could be a player or a drug user, hell, I don't know."

"Unbelievable," she said, standing. "Really, Kory, really? I am sorry for what you went through with Tressa, but trying to bad-mouth Colby when you don't know a thing about him is just plain crazy. What do you want from me, Kory? Tell me!" she yelled. "I am with Colby now and I am over you, okay? So if you want to be more than friends, we can't talk anymore, we can't hang, and I certainly cannot continue to be here for you."

He got to his feet. "Tiff, hold on, okay, calm down. We are friends and I care about you. I just don't want to see you get hurt, okay?"

"Look, Kory," she said, her eyes watering. "I don't want to kill our friendship, but in order for me to move on, it has to be done, because I can't do this."

He moved closer to her. "Tiff, please, I'm begging you not to walk out the door. I love you, Tiffany, and I want to be with you. I know that Colby is not the one for you. I know you love me too, so please, just stay and you and I can start on us. Take it one day at a time, and just make each other happy."

"No, Kory, no, we can't, okay?" She blinked back tears. "I am with Colby and I am happy with him. So please, just be happy for me, just as I was for you when you were with Tressa."

"Colby isn't the one, Tiff."

"How do you know?" she yelled. "Because you are free to move about the cabin now? Why can't you accept that he makes me happy?"

"Because Tressa paid him to go out with you!"

"What?" she asked in disbelief.

"Tressa paid him to go out with you. She sent him to your premiere party for *Boy Crazy* and paid him to woo you, so you would stay away from me."

She looked at him blankly. "Oh my God, Kory. Seriously? It has come to you making up shit about Colby to get me to stay with you?"

"I'm not lying, Tiff, Amber told me today. I didn't want to say anything, but you needed to know."

She stood frozen in disbelief. After she gathered her thoughts, she said, "You are a liar and I never want to see you, ever, ever again. If you come anywhere near me, God is my witness, I will scream bloody murder. How did you turn into this selfish, evil liar? You should have stayed with Tressa, because you two are one of a kind!" She put her glass down, stormed inside the house, grabbed her purse, and headed to the front door.

Kory ran after her, trying to reason with her, but she refused to stop and listen. She got into her car and he kept trying to talk to her, but she refused to listen.

"I'm not lying. I love you," he yelled as her tires shrieked out of his circular driveway.

Tiffany drove away fighting tears. The idea of Colby doing that to her was ridiculous; she couldn't believe Kory would stoop so low. When she arrived at Colby's house, she was surprised to see so many cars. She didn't understand why he didn't tell her he was throwing a party.

She made her way through the crowd and found him. She discovered a friend of his popped in from out of town and invited some folks over, who invited others. She didn't feel particularly welcome at his party and it didn't take her long to see that he had had one too many drinks. She mingled with a few of his guests, and when she saw Vi, she reminded him who she was.

They found a corner to chat and she asked him if he would do the theme song for her show for TiMax. He immediately agreed. She asked him to write it with Julia Valentine in mind, because she was sure she'd agree to do the vocals.

His reply was, "I'm all over it." He told her he had caught an episode or two and that he thought the show was a winner. He made sure she had his number and they made plans to meet another day.

She went to find her man and found him in a circle of young beautiful women. She remembered what he said about his ex, so she went over to the bar and got a drink and tried to not think about what Kory had said to her.

When the night finally came to an end, she found Colby passed out across his bed, still fully dressed.

"Colby," she whispered and tapped him.

"Yeah," he replied.

"I'm gonna go down and start cleaning."

He rolled over. "No, no, no, boo, come here. A cleaning crew is coming in the morning to handle that. Come give daddy what he needs."

She climbed on top of him and they kissed. She went for his belt and heard the raging sounds of snores coming from his nose, so she stopped. She looked up and saw he was out, mouth opened and all.

"No, no, this is not going down like this," she said.

She shook him and nothing. She sat up in his bed and kicked him until he rolled over, but it still didn't wake him. She was pissed and frustrated, but what could she do? She got up, wrote him a quick note, and left.

When she got into her ride, she thought about Kory and what he said, but shook it off. She tried to deny it, but she wanted to run back to his house. She knew that would not be good, so she hit the highway and headed home.

Chapter Twenty-three

The ringing phone woke Tiffany. It was Kory, so she hit IGNORE. She turned over and went back to sleep. Ten minutes later, he called again. She still didn't answer. Next, she got a text message that said, I'm sorry. She read it and put her phone back down. She gave up on sleeping, because all she could think of was Kory and what he had said about Colby.

What if he was telling the truth? Colby did just appear out of nowhere. How could he toy with her like that and pretend to be interested when he really wasn't. "All this 'take it slow' bullshit," she said. She got up and went to the bathroom. "Was sex not in your contract?" she murmured. She turned on the shower, angry as hell. She decided she was going to pay Tressa a visit. If she asked Colby straight out, he would just deny it or find a way to convince her that Kory had it all wrong.

She dressed and called Kory, hoping he'd tell her Tressa's location. When he answered, it took him more than fifteen minutes to finally give Tiffany what she called for.

When she got to the Green's estate she was stopped at the gate. "Yes, ma'am, can I help you?" the security guy at the gate asked.

"I am here to see Tressa. Can you tell her that it's Tiffany Richardson?"

"I'm sorry, Miss Richardson, but she isn't available. I will be sure to tell her you came by."

Tiffany wondered if he was making that up or if she was truly not at home. "Do you know where I can find her? It is kinda urgent."

"Well, she is out of town for a few days, ma'am."

She let out the breath she was holding. "Okay, thanks."

She put her car in drive and turned to leave the premises. She wondered where Tressa had gone and decided she had to go to Colby and confront him. She pulled out her phone and called him.

He answered on the first ring. "Hey, babe, what's up? I am so sorry about last night. I had no idea Des was coming into town. He just dropped by with his crew, and before I knew it, I had a li'l party going on."

"That's fine, Colby, I'm not trippin' on that."

"Okay, then what's up? I hear it in your voice. I know you're probably pissed because I passed out on you, but, babe, I swear I got up today with plans of making it up to you. I am thinking up a romantic evening for us as we speak. I planned to do you right tonight."

That didn't sound pleasant to her ears. Maybe if it would have come before the news of Tressa paying him to go out with her, it would have been nice. "Listen, there is something I really need to talk to you about. Can I come by?"

"Sure, babe, that's cool."

She headed in his direction. The closer she got to his house, the angrier she got. The idea of someone paying for someone to go out with her turned her stomach, like she was some ugly, dateless charity case or desperate. She pulled into Colby's driveway and gave herself a pep talk before she got out. She reminded herself not to be soft and to pay close attention to him. He was an actor, and now she felt like an innocent bystander in his and Tressa's sick movie.

She approached the house and he opened the door right away and greeted her with his normal soft kiss. "Look at you, beautiful," he said.

Put a sock in it, you liar, she thought. "Hey, Colby," she said dryly.

"Okay, boo, what's up? Why the long face? I said I'ma make it up to you."

She walked into the kitchen and stood on the other side of the island. He stood across from her and she looked him in the eyes. "Did Tressa Green pay you to go out with me?"

"Excuse me?" he said, blinking his eyes rapidly.

"Did Tressa Green pay you to go out with me?" she repeated in a firmer tone.

"Tiff, where did you hear that? Who told you that?" He looked at her like that was totally absurd.

"It doesn't matter, Colby. Is it true? Did she pay you to go out with me?"

"No." He had a look of disgust on his face. "Where did you hear that bullshit, baby? That is insane."

"A close source told Kory that Tressa paid you to go out with me to keep me away from him during their engagement."

"Kory said that? Kory? As in the Kory who is supposed to be just your friend from back in the day?"

"Yes." She wondered if Kory really did lie.

"Sounds like he wants to be more than friends to me." Colby moved closer to her.

"Why would he lie, Colby? Why would he make something like that up?"

"Listen, babe, that is ridiculous. I know Tressa, yes, who doesn't? We were at a party and she was ranting about this chick named Tiffany from her fiancé's past who was a thorn in her side. She goes on and on about you being the executive producer of the show, and the next couple days, I get an invite to your premiere. I went, laid eyes on you when you were giving your speech, and I wanted to get to know you.

"It had nothing to do with Tressa, so whoever told Kory that bullshit lied, babe. It's no secret that we're dating. Maybe she was talking shit to a group of people like she usually does and said she had to pay me to go out with you to be facetious and make you look bad, babe. I would never let someone talk me into no bullshit like that, boo."

She let him embrace her. He sounded sincere and she believed him. Tressa was a popular party girl with a big mouth and she was capable of saying and doing evil things like that and her groupies and fans would believe her. "So not a

word of that is true? You didn't make any contract or agreement with her to go out with me?"

"Babe, no," he said and kissed her. "You are
too fine, too smart, and it is my pleasure to be
your man." He kissed her deeply and grabbed
her ass. She felt his erection through his pants.
"You wanna take this upstairs?" he asked.

She looked at him one more time to see if she
could detect a hint of bullshit, but he seemed
sincere. "Lead the way," she said.

He took her by the hand and led her to his
room. She stripped down quickly to her undies,
not ashamed of her hourglass figure. She wasn't
fat at all, and she was thick in all the right
places. Her waist was slim, her breasts were
perky, and her hips and ass were rounded perfectly. She was between a twelve and fourteen,
but her body was shapely and she knew she
looked good in her matching panties and bra.

Colby stepped out of his shorts. She could
see his bulge underneath his boxer briefs,
and it was swollen well. He pulled his tank
over his head, exposing his chiseled chest and
eight-pack stomach. It didn't take long for her
pussy to release the natural moisture that she
seemed to get whenever he got close to her
lately.

"Are you sure you want to do this, babe?" he
asked. "Because it's not about sex for me."

She believed him. He was the first man she'd ever dated who wasn't itching to get into her panties.

"Stop talking," she said.

She went on her toes and put her arms around his neck and they kissed. He caressed her skin and grabbed her ass and she enjoyed the way his tongue danced around hers. He rubbed her back before unhooking her bra, freeing her perfectly round breasts with their hard, dark nipples. He pushed her panties away from her body and then pushed his boxers down while she climbed into his bed.

Tiffany never gave oral on her first sexual encounter, but the way Colby licked her down her neck and gave gratifying suction to her nipples, she felt as if she was going to be in a pleasure match.

She didn't ask him, but she didn't stop him from going down farther. He stopped, got up, wrapped his arms firmly around her thighs, and pulled her pussy to his face. He began to please her clit with his tongue and she couldn't hold back her moans. He was definitely good at what he was doing. In no time, she climaxed and begged him to release her.

He complied and sat up, stroking his dick in his hand and looking at her. His mushroomed head looked sexy as hell and Tiffany wanted it to be near her cervix, so she told him to hurry.

"I am, baby, just a sec."

He grabbed a condom and she couldn't wait for him to roll it on. When he was ready, he pushed her legs apart and slowly entered. She closed her eyes and released a sexy sound to let him know she was happy to have him inside of her. He found his rhythm and she lay there and enjoyed the deep strokes of his perfect dick. It was definitely the right fit, because it filled her up each time he pushed forward.

"Yes, baby, yes," she whispered with her eyes closed.

"Oooh, Tiff, baby, you feel so good."

He pushed her legs open a little wider and pulled her closer to the edge of the bed so he could go a little deeper. He bent his knees slightly and went so deep that her moans changed from oohs to aahs. She was getting wetter by the stroke. She opened her eyes to look at her lover. He looked into her eyes and kissed her, his tongue tangling with hers.

He pulled out. "Slide back," he said softly and she did.

He checked to make sure the condom was still on properly and when she opened up for him again, he slipped back in. He pressed his lean body onto hers and pumped her steadily, giving her a couple kisses on her forehead before he got back to her lips.

He started to passionately kiss her again, and when he began to suck on her tongue, it heightened the sensation for her and she began to roll it back on him.

"That's good, aaaahhhh, that's good," he said between breaths.

She pulled him close and wrapped her arms and legs around his body. He pressed deeper and deeper and she moaned a sweet sound in his ear.

"Get it, baby, get it," she said, cheering him on. It was damn good. Her clit began to tingle, and she climaxed again.

"Turn over and get on your knees," he said, pulling out again.

"I'm sorry," she said when she saw the huge wet spot. They laughed.

"Boo, that is definitely not a reason to be sorry," he joked as they got into position. He pulled her back a little bit by her hips and positioned her ass the way he wanted it. He went in, pumped a couple times and paused, and then he pumped a couple more times and pulled out.

"What's wrong?" she asked, knowing damn well what that meant. She wasn't new at this.

"It's right there," he said and gave her a couple gentle kisses on her back. "I want it to last a little longer before I nut."

She let him take a couple moments. He re-entered her and after a few pumps he squeezed her hips tightly and pumped eight or nine fast ones before he stopped. He rested on her back a couple seconds and then slowly pulled out.

"Tiffany, Tiffany, Tiffany. Girl, you got some good stuff. Where have you been all my life?" he teased.

"Where have you been all my life?" she returned.

He went to the master bathroom to flush the latex and she lay down and took a couple deep breaths. When he returned, he climbed in, got behind her, and pulled her body closer to his. He gave her a couple gentle kisses on her shoulder before he rested his head on a pillow.

"Baby, that was amazing," he said.

"It was," she said, smiling.

"What the hell was I waiting on?"

"Beats me. I honestly thought you were gay or had a little bitty dick," she said holding up two fingers with a little space between them.

"Wrong on both," he said and they laughed.

She locked her fingers into his. "And I'm so glad I was."

"Listen, why don't you go home, shower, put on something fierce, and pack a bag," he suggested.

"Pack a bag for?"

"I don't know yet, babe, but I'm going to call my travel agent and find someplace to fly you."

"You don't have to do that, Colby. I only have a couple more weeks before we get back to work on the show." A getaway sounded good, but she wanted to spend the next few days bouncing around show ideas.

"I want to, Tiffany. I want to do something nice for you."

"I have to work, Colby," she said.

"Work? You have a couple weeks before the show gets underway," he protested.

"I don't technically have to go in, but I want to start noting some ideas, you know."

"Okay, how about I take you somewhere relaxing, where you can do your show thing *and* have a li'l fun with me?" He started kissing her on her neck.

"Okay, I guess that will work. And I wanted to know if you'd mind coming on the show as a guest star or even joining the show."

"That sounds great, but I will have to decline on that."

"Why? That would be great, Colby. I mean, you are an A-list actor and you would make an impact on the ratings, you know."

"Listen, Tiff, it sounds great, and I'd do anything to make you happy, but I like what we have and I want to keep our relationship as it is, not businesslike, okay? We are doing fine, and the moment we may not be doing fine, work becomes an issue. So, no. I'll be happy to make a guest appearance and whatnot, but no contract, nothing permanent. I do not want to jinx this, babe. Your show is going to be a success and your ratings are going to go through the roof without me."

She kissed the back of his hand. "You're right, babe, and I'm sorry. Just promise me that you'll come on an episode or two."

"I promise. Now get your sexy ass up and ride my dick before you go."

She felt his erection flex against her ass and she turned over to look at him. "Damn, you gon' just ask a sista like that?"

"I'm sorry, allow me to rephrase. Will you do me the honor of getting your sexy ass on top of me and slowly coming down on my penis and riding it for a spell?" he asked in a British accent.

She burst into laughter. "It would be my pleasure, sir," she mimicked with the same accent.

He paused to get another condom. They got it in and she didn't want to move, but she had to go.

She headed home. When she pulled up to her house, she saw Kory's Bentley. Then she saw him. *Why is this fool sitting on my porch?* she thought.

Chapter Twenty-four

"What, Kory?" she yelled as soon as she slammed her car door shut. "Why are you here?" He was the last person she wanted to see. When she checked her phone, he had called her ten times while she was getting served by Colby.

"We need to talk, Tiff," he said, standing.

As mad as she was at him for lying on Colby, she wondered why the fuck he always looked so damn good. "No, we don't," she said. She wished he didn't make her stomach do flips every time she saw him.

"We do, Tiff. I didn't tell you about Colby to hurt you. I only wanted to warn you. I don't want to see you hurt."

She knew that Kory wouldn't lie to be malicious. He had just gotten the wrong information. "Kory, it's not true. Tressa didn't pay Colby, okay? Amber got her facts wrong. Colby is not that guy, okay? I appreciate your concern and I thank you for trying to look out for me, but Colby is a great guy and I really, really like him. I wish that you would stay away and let me be." She looked away, hoping he'd just leave her alone so she could get on with her life. He didn't say anything, but she could feel him looking at her. "Listen, I'm sorry things didn't work out with you and Tressa, but it would be best if we didn't hang out or be friends."

"Tiff, listen, okay? I know it may be hard to believe, but Amber would have never told me if it weren't true. She and Amber have been friends forever, and she only told me so I could warn you."

Tiffany didn't want to hear another word. "Stop, okay, Kory, stop. Why are you doing this, huh? Why the fuck are you pushing this? What do you want me to do? Say 'Kory, you're right and you and I are going to be together' Or . . . or . . . or we can pick up where we never left off?" She held back her tears. She had accepted that they would never be when he left that night to go back to Tressa. "When I saw you that day at that restaurant, I thought, 'My God, this has got to be fate,' and I could not get you out of my mind. We sat there and talked and caught up, but not once did you open your mouth and say, 'I'm engaged to be married.' When I asked you to meet me for dinner, you still led me like a blind horse to water.

"You came here the night of your engagement party and made out with me, and still ran back to Tressa. So get off my damn porch. Go home and find a way to get over this. I left you alone to be with Tressa, so leave me alone so I can be with Colby."

She was not going to be torn between two men. She had been reunited with Kory, the love of her life, and it was just bad timing. Now she had a chance to be with someone who adored her and she wasn't going to let Kory walk back into her life at his own convenience. It was not going to work like that.

"Tiff, I can truly understand how you feel and where you are coming from. You are right; that day at the café, I should have said something. But you know what? I was taken back and the memories of you resurfaced in my brain in an instant and I couldn't let the words part from my lips. I wanted to. I . . . I did, but I thought if I said that, you'd go off and I'd never see you again. The night you asked me to dinner, I honestly had no intention of bringing Tressa. I just wanted to see you and reminisce, talk about home and all that jazz, and I was going to tell you.

"Tressa insisted that she go, and I didn't have time to call to warn you, because I didn't want to start shit with her. To warn you would have made me look guilty, so I just prayed you wouldn't mind. I don't know Colby like you do, Tiff, and if you believe him, there is nothing left to say. Take care, and I won't bother you or contact you again if that's the way you want it."

He turned and walked down the four steps. He headed to his car and Tiffany stood on the porch confused. Kory was a sweetheart, a gentleman, and she knew he meant well. She knew he only left her to honor his commitment to Tressa, but it was much too late. She and Colby were an item now, and even though she wasn't in love with him, she liked him enough to want to stay.

She watched Kory's taillights hit the corner, and when he turned, she went inside. She went for her travel bag and grabbed a couple summer dresses and laid them on her bed. The dresses were comfortable, cute, and could be worn for just about any occasion. As long as they went somewhere warm, she'd be good. She grabbed three pairs of her cute sandals with a small heel and went for her travel toiletry bag. It had all of the essentials, and if she needed something other than that, she'd buy it. She started the shower, and as she lathered she couldn't stop thinking about Kory.

She felt bad for him and knew he had to be going through a tough time because of the breakup. Even though they had made out and came close to having sex, apparently his feelings for Tressa kept him from staying with her that night. She hated that she had found such a great guy like Colby, while he had love lost.

When she got out of the shower, she was tempted to call him to say they could still be friends, but just as soon as she was dressed, the doorbell rang. She knew it could only be Colby. At least she hoped, because Kory had frequently dropped by without calling.

"Hey," she said when she opened the door and saw Colby.

He leaned in with a kiss. "Hey, are you ready to go?"

"Yes, I am," she said going toward her room to get her bag. "Where are you taking me?"

"It's a surprise."

"Okay now, Colby, I only packed a couple sundresses," she warned.

"And if you need anything other than those, we will buy something. Honestly, I was hoping you only packed sexy underwear," he joked.

"Don't worry, I packed those too." She gave him a sexy smile. "Now, can we get this show on the road?"

"Sure, after you." He followed her to the front door.

They left for the airport, and even though he tried to be secretive, it didn't take her long to figure out where they were going.

"Vegas, Colby? Didn't I tell you I wanted quiet and relaxation?"

He smiled. "And you will have that, my dear. We are staying at the Bellagio and there are plenty of relaxing and peaceful things you can do while I hit the tables. We can get in a show or two, of course some great food, and then fuck until we can't move."

She slapped his arm. "Not so loud," she warned. They were still in an airport.

"And then fuck until we can't move," he whispered. She laughed.

They both looked up at the exact same time and noticed two white girls standing by.

"Are you Colby Grant?" one asked. She looked like she was going to come out of her skin.

Colby did a sexy smile. He had his baseball cap low and his dark shades, but he was still recognizable. "If I say yes, will you young ladies keep your cool and not alert the rest of the ticket holders for this flight?"

"We promise," the other said, pen in hand. "All we want is an autograph and a picture with you for our Facebook page, and I promise we will move on."

When the girls had gotten what they came for, Tiffany suggested they head to the VIP lounge until it was time to board and Colby agreed.

"Okay, Mr. Superstar," she teased, once they found a place at the bar.

"Awww babe, don't trip. This is nothing. L.A. folks don't get excited. It's other cities that will not stop following you through the airport. L.A. sees stars in the airport like they see stars in the sky."

"I guess you're right. I ain't trippin', and I'm certainly not jealous of those two teenagers," she added.

"That's good, because you don't have to be. And they did look over twenty-one to me." he joked.

She gave him the "really?" look.

"It doesn't matter anyway. I'm with who I want to be with and I'm good."

"Are you sure? Because I'm just Tiffany, plain ol' Tiffany." She smiled. "What you see is what you get."

"Damn, what I see is all I want." He leaned in and kissed her.

They ordered and the barmaid knew who Colby was too, but she played it cool. When she gave Colby his ticket, she made sure her number was written on it. Tiffany didn't trip or say anything, because she didn't blame a girl for trying; however, she was happy to see Colby toss the receipt before they boarded the plane. First class was always nice, so she sat back and enjoyed the flight.

Chapter Twenty-five

"Okay, people, we are back, and I must say I am glad to be back," Tiffany said to her writers. They were in their very first meeting to discuss getting the show back into production at TiMax. "We have like a million and one things to do and not a lot of time to do it in, so we gotta put our game face on and get it done." Everyone in the room applauded. The room hummed with excitement and she knew they were anxious to get to work.

"Okay, I know today is our first day, but we have a lot to cover and we are going to be here for a while, so be prepared to take in a lot of information today. Everyone has their new tablet in front of them. We are going to go through a few slides and go over cast, budget, and then the show's direction. Miss Dallas, here, is going to give us a tour of the entire studio and then we are going to get to see our new set. Over the next couple days, we are going to get acquainted with the set decorator, scene designer, set construction crew, lighting, prop masters, sound, and art director. Now, when we go to our new set, have your notepads ready, because we are going to have to picture scenes and y'all already know. This is not our first rodeo ride, so kindly write your names—legibly; Darryl, not that fancy stuff you be signing memos with—so others that don't know us can get familiar with who we are."

The group finished their meeting and got a tour of the entire studio. They finally pulled up to their lot so that they could walk onto their new set.

"Now, you guys can stay here as long as you need and give the front a call when you are ready for us to bring the carts back to get you guys," Dallas said.

"Thanks," Tiffany told her. "Wow," she said, looking around. "This is like five times bigger than our old set." She was so excited she felt her face getting hot.

"Yes, it is," Darrel said and everyone agreed.

"Okay, peeps, let's walk around, check things out, and don't be ashamed to be as creative as you can. We have to make KCLN look like skid row," she said.

After an hour or so, they rejoined each other and started shooting ideas like they normally did. Tiffany approved most, but scrunched her nose to indicate those she didn't like. They went back to the main office and she got right back to business. It had been four hours since they started, but it felt longer.

"I know everyone is anxious to grab lunch, but I want to give you guys a rundown on some show ideas, and then we break for lunch and get back to it." The group turned their attention to her. "So, now college is done and the girls are home. Of course, they have to go back to their parents and the first episode I want them to go apartment hunting. Of course, they are broke, so the places they see are dumps, but a miracle happens, so they think. Claire, since she is the wealthiest one, gets the news her favorite aunt died and left her some property that turns out to be kick-ass. The girls decide to move in together since there is no mortgage to be paid, but at say the end of the show, the power is cut off, and they have to find jobs to maintain the utilities."

She looked around to make sure her staff was taking notes. "Now, we have a huge budget and can hire a total of eight new cast members. So we have to create no more than eight new personalities to join this cast." Darryl held up his stylus. "Shoot," she said, giving him the floor.

"A nosy elderly neighbor who is always inter-fering with their lives," he suggested. Tiff gave the approval nod.

"A lazy super who never wants to fix things," Marsha blurted.

Tiff gave another nod. She waited for more, but no one said anything. She decided to call 'em out. "Alvin," she called.

He quickly came up with a new character. "Sexy bartender at their new hot spot, but he turns out to be gay and the girls find that out after they all go behind one another's back trying to hook up with him after they vowed he was off-limits." When he stopped speaking, he looked around like he had amazed himself.

"That's good, Alvin, nice. I like that idea. Liz," she called out, moving to the next person.

"Well, how about a therapist for Claire?" she asked nervously. "No way she will be able to handle her new life, she is horrible under pres-sure."

"And I've just learned that you're not," Tiffany said with a smile. "Now we've got room for four more and we don't have to cram, you guys. I know we are capable of getting this done. We've written a season in a matter of days because you guys rock, so instead of lunch, go home, come up with some witty ideas, and keep in mind that boys will come and go and we are not going to let our girls get serious in the first season, because that would be the end of our show. Note: profanity is allowed now and so is nudity, but keep in mind that there are to be no girl-on-girl scenes or scenarios. That is specified in all of the girls' contracts.

"Lastly, the girls are not afraid of nude scenes, and if, for comedy's sake, we can have a lesbian episode with someone trying to make Joy their bitch and she is clueless, that would be hilarious," she said laughing.

The crew agreed. Joy was the conservative one and was always scared to try or do anything. She was safe, so that would be a cute episode. Everyone was about to exit the room when Tiffany remembered one more thing.

"Oh, and guys, our show is an hour-long, commercial-free series now, so we gotta hit it. This is not a twenty-two-minute walk in the park. So are y'all ready to do this?" They nodded and she knew they were. "Y'all better be; that pay increase wasn't because y'all look good," she teased before they left.

When everyone was gone, she walked around her new think tank, which was just as upscale as the rest of the building. She didn't want to check the cabinets and fridge out in front of everyone, but she did so as soon as she was alone. She gathered her things to leave and decided to stop by her office. When she got there, she saw Myah. She had forgotten all about her assistant being there.

"Mee-Mee," she said.

Myah looked up from her novel and smiled. "How was the first day, Tiff?"

"It was full, I'll tell you. How about yours?"

"Quiet, the most quiet I've ever had. I'm almost finished with this book I started this morning. The phone rang once and they had the wrong number. I ordered lunch, and can you believe they have someone bring it up here to your desk?" She grinned from ear to ear. "I'm going to love it here."

Tiffany knew exactly what she meant. "You ain't seen nothing, girl, follow me."

She led her assistant into her office and shut the door. She went straight for the glasses and poured them both a drink. "Stocked with my favorite," she said and handed Myah a glass.

"If I'm not at my desk when you need me, I'll be right here," Myah said. They clinked glasses.

"Myah, this place is just too good to be true. I can't wait to get the show going." Tiffany took a seat at her desk. "I mean, I feel so accomplished and we haven't even recorded one episode yet." She took a sip.

"Tiffany, you deserve this," Myah told her. "You've worked hard and did in a little time what it takes others years to do. So bask in it, girl. This is your moment."

The two chatted for a while and had another drink. After a while, they decided it was time to leave, but before they could exit, there was a knock at the door.

"Come in," she said. To her surprise, it was Mr. Green.

"Hey, Miss Richardson. I'm so glad I caught you. Do you have a moment?" he asked.

"Sure, of course. This is my assistant, Myah. Myah, this is Mr. Green, our new boss. The network's owner."

Myah hurried over to shake his hand. "Nice to meet you, sir, and thank you so much for this opportunity."

"No problem, Myah. Welcome aboard," he said.

Maya told Tiffany good night and made her exit.

"May I?" Mr. Green asked, pointing to a chair.

"Of course. What brings you by?"

"I just wanted to stop in and give you a proper welcome. I hope everything is to your liking."

She smiled. "Yes, everything is more than great, and the staff here has made me and my cast and crew feel very welcome."

"That is terrific. I am anxious to see you in action. I admire your drive, Tiffany. You're the daughter I never had."

Tiffany wasn't sure how to reply. "Yeah, well, I know where you are coming from. I've met your daughter," she joked.

"Yes, Isabella was and still is a handful."

"Who?" she asked, confused.

"I'm sorry, Tressa. Isabella is her middle name. Her momma and I argued and argued about naming our first and only child and finally, we flipped a coin. Heads was Isabella, tails was Tressa. And as you can see, tails was a winner."

"Well, I like both," she said, being nice. She didn't want to insult his family.

"Me too, and as soon as my daughter and Kory are married, she will be his handful." He chuckled.

Tiffany wasn't sure she heard him correctly. The last she knew, the engagement was off. "Married?" she asked.

"Yes, I'm so anxious to give her away. I think Kory can help her to get on the straight and narrow. I see so many qualities in that young man. How the miracle of him falling for my spoiled daughter happened, I don't know, but I am so glad it did."

"Yes, Kory is one of the good ones."

"As I heard it, you and he used to be an item."

"No, sir, nothing like that. We've always been friends, but never dated," she said, clearing it up.

"That's strange. Isabella gave me an entirely different story of your history with Kory."

"Well, sir, you can ask Kory if you'd like. We sorta grew up together, went to high school together, and that was pretty much it. His cousin and I used to be friends, but Kory and I, we never got together."

"Son of a bitch," he said out loud. "That daughter of mine is certainly a character. She should have a series of her own," he joked. "She has always had a way with me. For so long, I've tried to be firm with Tressa, but my heart goes to mush. I've been delaying her trust, hoping she'd get some type of act right, but, hey . . ." He cleared his throat. "That's not why I came by. I came by to welcome you and to wish you well. I am sure you're going to rock TiMax, and I look forward to seeing what you do with the show. If at any time you need anything, let me know."

"Thank you, Mr. Green, and I won't disappoint you," she said.

"I know you won't. Enjoy the rest of your day, Miss Richardson," he said and went to stand, but he sat back down.

Concerned, Tiffany asked, "Mr. Green, are you all right?"

He smiled, but held his chest and took a few deep breaths. "I'm okay. Just been super busy here lately and I may need a mini vacation."

"Can I get you some water? You look flushed."

"Yes, please." Tiffany hurried over to get him a bottle of water. She opened it and handed it to him. She watched him take a few swallows.

"Should I call someone? Tressa or your wife?"

"No, no, no. I don't want to worry them. I mean my wife is always on me about my diet and I know I take my job a little too serious. I'll be fine, just need to lose some of my workload." He smiled.

His color started to look normal again, and he did a clean swipe with is handkerchief to clean the beads of sweat from his head.

"Are you sure, Mr. Green? I mean our health is a serious thing."

"I'm sure. I'm fine." He stood and put the remainder of water on Tiffany's desk and headed for the door. Tiffany smiled when he turned to her. "Let's just keep this between us okay?"

"Will do, sir." He headed out the door and Tiffany went to gather her things. She didn't know what was going on, but she hoped he was okay.

Maybe that was why Tressa still hadn't told him that the wedding was off. Maybe she was concerned about his health? She wondered if she should call Kory, but immediately told herself to stay out of it. She didn't want to go sticking her nose where it didn't belong.

She grabbed her purse and briefcase and headed home.

Chapter Twenty-six

Tiffany was present as the construction crew worked nonstop on the set her show would be taping their new season on. She occasionally interrupted, but not much because they had her vision under control. The cast came by daily to read through the scripts and agreed or disagreed and gave the writers their input to make the character feel like their character. They were doing casting calls and scene adjustments, and she wasn't sure they'd be ready to start taping in time. She had her doubts, but her crew and staff always assured her things would fall into place.

She was working later and later, so she didn't have much time to spend with Colby, and she missed him. She promised him that she'd meet him for dinner that night and would bring an overnight bag to spend the night. She couldn't wait.

Once her day came to an end, she headed to her office and ran into Tressa. She wondered why she was hanging around the station when she didn't work there.

"Tiffany, nice to see you," she said with a smile fake as the solar nails Tiffany had on her fingertips.

"Hello, Tressa how are you?" Tiffany returned dryly and tried to keep going.

"I'm great, never been better. Just planning my wedding and living in bliss."

Tiffany laughed.

"Did I say something to amuse you?" Tressa asked smartly.

"I just thought I heard you say you were planning your wedding, the wedding I heard from the groom is off."

"Well, you may have heard that it was off, but it's not. Kory just needs a moment and I'm giving him that. But I can assure you, Miss Richardson, Kory and I will be married."

"Okay," Tiffany said and started walking away. She wasn't in any mood to deal with Tressa.

"Think what you want to think, Tiffany. I got this under control and trust, sweetie pie, Kory and I will be married."

"If you say so." Tiffany went on to her office and gathered her things to leave.

When she got into her car and was headed toward Colby's, she couldn't resist calling Kory.

"Hello," he said.

"Hey, Kory, this is Tiff." She swallowed hard. "Do you have a moment?"

"Sure, what's up?"

"I just have a quick question."

"Okay," he said.

"Are you and Tressa back together again?"

"No, why do you ask?"

"Because she is still planning your wedding."

"What makes you think that?"

"I ran into her a few moments ago and she said she was still wedding planning and that you and she were still going to tie the knot."

"Well, that's not true. I haven't spoken to Tressa at all."

"Well, apparently she thinks you guys are still on, and she hasn't even told her folks that the wedding is off."

"How do you know all this?"

"Because a couple weeks ago Mr. Green came into my office talking about you taking over the burden of his troublesome daughter. The man has no clue you called the wedding off." Kory was silent. "Hello?" she said.

"I'm here," he said. "I just don't know what to say. I mean, I thought it would be best if the news came from Tressa, but I guess I'll have to tell Mr. Green myself."

"Well, that's the only way he'll know, because Tressa is not going to be the one to tell him. That's for sure."

"I guess not. So how are you, Tiff? How is the show stuff going?"

"It's going. Man, and I have been super busy. The studio, the production, the entire thing is like ten times bigger than it was at KCLN, so it's been early mornings and very late nights for me."

"So how has the superstar been able to deal with it?"

"Superstar?" she asked confused.

"Mr. Movie Star, Colby?"

"He's not happy, but he understands. He knows the industry, so he is being supportive."

"Really? Maybe he does care about you for real."

"Kory, please don't. Don't start that shit again."

"What shit?"

"That bullshit about him being paid to sleep with me."

"Oh, so you're sleeping with him now?"

"You know what I meant, Kory." She couldn't believe she'd said the words "sleep with" and not "go out with."

"Yeah, I gotta go," he said and hung up in her face.

Tiffany was shocked. Why was he trippin'? He knew Colby was her man, and eventually they'd sleep together. She started to call him back, but Colby called her.

"Hey, you, I'm on my way," she said when she answered.

"Hey, that's why I'm calling you. I need a rain check. I had this thing with my agent come up and I'm about to head out and meet him."

"Colby, really? It's been days since I saw you last."

"I know, I know, but duty calls. You know how it goes, babe. There's going to be some directors and screenwriters at this gig and I gotta go. You know, to rub some elbows."

"I know, but I'm not happy," she whined.

"Tomorrow, I promise," he said "Tomorrow."

She agreed. When they hung up, she got off the road and turned around and headed home. She could have stayed at work if she knew he'd cancel.

"Oh, well," she said and drove toward her place.

She stopped at a drive thru and got a salad. When she got home, she felt lonely. She thought of Colby, but not as much as she thought of Kory. She wanted to call him just to talk, but what would she say? What would be her reason to call him, she wondered as she dumped the half-eaten soggy salad into the trash.

She went to shower, but looked at her tub and decided to take a hot bath. She poured herself a glass of red and grabbed her iPod and put it on the dock in her bathroom. She went to Fantasia again, but then decided to listen to Chrisette Michele instead.

She slid into the tub and kept looking at her phone. She wanted to call Kory so badly, but she fought the urge. She drank her wine slowly and when the water began to cool, she grabbed her sponge and body wash and lathered up. She got out, dried her skin, and did her lotion routine and put on a short, comfortable cotton nightgown.

She slid her feet into her slippers, went into the kitchen, poured another drink, and opened the sliding door to her deck off the kitchen. She normally sat on her little patio off her bedroom, but tonight she wanted a different atmosphere. She wondered how she could be so crazy about Colby and still yearn for Kory.

She ran back inside, grabbed her phone and said, "No, no, Tiffany, don't." It was a struggle, but she didn't make that call.

Chapter Twenty-seven

Rehearsals came quickly and the set was done. Five weeks had gone by and they were all a blur. Tiffany could count on one hand how often she saw Colby. They were always missing each other, and now that he had a role on a new television series, he was working just as much as she was. They'd have time for a quick dinner or a quickie at her place or his, but there was no staying all night and no time spent together. Colby was a huge romantic, he stayed up on sending flowers and little gifts, but she missed him and couldn't care less about the flowers, cards, candy, and jewelry.

As the show progressed, her love life was relegated to text messages, e-mails, and voice messages. She wondered if she and Colby should just have called it quits, because the hour or two visits weren't cutting it for her.

Now, it was taping time. The show was on schedule and everyone was elated. The sex scenes and nudity were a challenge at first, but they had a crew of greats working with them, so things were going well. Mr. Green joined a couple tapings and he was always happy with what he saw when the director said, "Clear."

Tiffany could tell he was really fond of her and she could see his mood shift whenever Tressa stepped into the room. She kept watching the other girl, wondering when she was going to tell her father that the wedding was off. The date was drawing near, and since Kory hadn't stepped up and told Mr. Green that he called it off, Mr. Green was still walking around thinking he would be giving his daughter away in a few weeks.

"Daddy, do you have a second?" Tressa interrupted.

"In a minute," he said and continued his conversation with Tiffany. "That cooking scene was brilliant. I mean it was hilarious, reminded me of an episode of *I Love Lucy*."

"And that was exactly what we were going for, Mr. Green. You know these girls can't cook, but women will do anything to impress a man." Tiffany nudged him and they both laughed. Mr. Green continued to laugh and joke with her, and Tiffany could see the irritation written all over his daughter's face. "Well, I'll let you get to your daughter. I'll see you on set tomorrow, right?" Tiffany leaned in to give him a quick hug and he gave her a quick peck on the cheek.

"Yes, I wouldn't miss it," he said.

Enraged, Tressa watched Tiffany walk away.

"Yes, Isabella," her father said. She noticed his tone was different from the one he'd used with Tiffany.

"Well, I just came by to see if you had a moment to chat about some wedding things."

"Me? I thought you and your mother had that under control." He began to walk and she took a couple of quick steps to catch up with him.

"Ummm, we do, Dad, but there are some masculine touches I want to add for Kory, and I wanted your opinion." She followed him out to a cart.

"Well, why don't you ask Kory? It's his wedding, not mine." They climbed into the cart and the driver took off.

"I would, Daddy, but I wanted to surprise him, you know?"

Mr. Green paused before he spoke. "Okay then, what? What do you want my input on?"

She hadn't expected him to give in, so she made up something. "Well, the groom's cake.

Kory likes golfing and fishing, so I was thinking a cake shaped into clubs or a cake that looks like a big fish." Her dad laughed. "What, Daddy?" she asked, confused.

"I say clubs. I wouldn't want to eat a cake that looks like a fish. And you know you don't need my input on this, Isabella, so why are you really here?" he asked.

She stuck to her story. "Daddy, come on. I value your opinion and I appreciate your style, so I do want to get your input."

Not convinced he said, "Okay, what else do you want to ask me?"

"About gifts for the groomsmen. I thought I'd give them all cologne, but you know everything ain't for everybody, so what do you suggest?"

"Watches. A nice watch works for a man."

Tressa smiled. "Daddy, that is a great idea." The cart pulled up to the main building and they got out.

"You've never asked my opinion on anything; you and your mother have always done these things. So again I ask, what do you really want, Isa? I'm a busy man and I have things to do." They reached the door to the building and he opened it for her.

Still acting innocent, she said, "Daddy, why are you so suspicious?"

"Because I know you. Now come on with it. Spit it out. Did you convince your mother to go over budget? Did you spend way more than I said on your dress? I know it's something, Isa," he said a little impatient. He knew Tressa like the back of his hand and she was pushing him closer to his grave. He'd been through more than a father should with her and he couldn't wait to marry her off. Give her her trust and then she'd be Kory's problem and he and his wife could have some peace.

His marriage was perfect and he and his wife got along great, but Tressa was what drove a wedge between them. He spoiled her too much and his wife complained; she spoiled her too much and he complained. At the end of the day, Tressa was always the reason they had issues in their marriage.

"Well, Daddy, to be honest, I came here to talk to you about my place at TiMax." Her words came out in a rush. "Daddy, I think it's time you showed me the ropes. I mean, you don't have a son or any other children that Mom and I know of, and you are not going to live forever."

He hit the up button for the elevator and the doors opened. They stepped in and he said, "Oh, so now you are putting me in the ground?"

"No, Daddy, it's not like that. I just want some power and control at this company, and I think it's unfair that you won't give me a chance."

"Isabella, Isabella, Isabella. You don't have a head for business. This is my baby. Me and Mike started this company from nothing, and even if I died tomorrow, you will never have control of this company. You have not shown me any ounce of responsibility. You have a condo on the beach, yet you're home, in your old room. Unless you're partying and don't want me and your mother to see you wasted. Just get married, have a couple children, and show us—me and your mother—that you care about the important things. Then and only then will I change my mind."

Tressa's anger was kindled and she didn't hide it. The elevator doors opened and they got out. "So that's it? You are treating me like I don't have your blood running through my veins. You are going to act as if I haven't changed, Daddy, huh?" she yelled.

"Lower your voice!" he demanded. He hurried into his office and she was right on his heels.

"No, I will not. I want you to look at me, Daddy and, admit that I've changed."

"Isa, it's been five minutes since you've been the new you and that isn't long enough for me to just trust you working here. I keep telling you to focus on getting married."

"It sounds like you are just trying to pawn me off."

He paused before he spoke. "That's not true, but I think marriage will be the best thing for you. Tressa, you are just not cut out for business. Everything you've sought out to do you had to come to me to save it, pay it off because you didn't make good on it, or you've just plain ol' lost the endorsement because of your reckless-ness. Get married okay? At least accomplish that," he said and poured himself a drink. He took a swallow and waited for his daughter to make another plea for respect and responsibility, neither of which she deserved.

"Fuck you, Daddy," she belted.

Shocked, he said, "Isa, are you insane?"

"No, Daddy, I'm not! You kiss Tiffany Richardson's ass every single day like she is your daughter and not me, and I don't give a shit anymore!" she blasted.

Mr. Green grabbed his chest and started to gasp for air and he then dropped the glass. He went down.

"Daddy? Oh my God, Daddy," she said and rushed over to him.

"Call nine-one-one," he struggled to say.

Tressa panicked and yelled for help. Her dad's receptionist came running in. "Call nine-one-one now!" she yelled when she saw her. "It's okay, Daddy, it's okay!" she cried and held him. "Please, Daddy, I'm so sorry. Please don't die on me. Please," she begged.

Paramedics were there within minutes. This was what she dreaded. Her daddy had a heart attack and she hoped to God that he survived it.

Chapter Twenty-eight

Tressa rode to the hospital in the ambulance with her dad. She called her mom on the way. They found out her daddy had suffered a massive heart attack and he was going to be out of commission for a while.

When her dad was finally able to come home, he knew he had to take it easy for a while and that meant no work. Tressa was now in control, because her mother didn't handle any business matters and after fifty years of being in the United States, she still didn't speak good English. She just stayed by her husband's side and did everything Tressa translated for her to do, including giving her dad a pill that the doctor didn't actually prescribe.

It was a downer, nothing life-threatening, but if it was Tressa thought it would be even better, because after she got over the shock of him having a heart attack, her evil mind figured she'd have control of everything if he was gone. She kissed her father good-bye that morning about twenty minutes after she gave him the sedative. He was too out of it, even if she hadn't given him the sleeping pill, to even dispute her saying she was going into the studio to work in his place. She was dressed to kill and she was going into the office to make heads spin.

She checked her mirror and reapplied her lipstick as all the executives came into the main conference room. She took a deep, cleansing breath and took her father's position at the head of the table. "Welcome, ladies and gentlemen. As you all know, my father has recently become ill. I will be standing in his place until his return." Everyone began to whisper. "No need for side-bars, it's true. The first thing on the agenda this morning is *Boy Crazy*." All eyes turned to her. "The show will be shut down until further notice," she said.

One of her father's associates laughed and she turned to him. "You're laughing because?" she asked him.

"Because you are a joke," he said. Everyone nodded in agreement. "Your father would have never given you any power to do a damn thing. Everyone in this room knows he doesn't want you anywhere near this company, on the board or even as a janitor. Unless you have an affidavit signed by Mr. Green saying otherwise, this meeting is adjourned. Meaning you can go home and take off your fancy little 'I'm in charge' suit," he said, doing air quotes. "And we will be getting back to work." He got up and everyone in the room followed suit.

Tressa was furious at the fact that they didn't take her seriously. She knew she had to come back with an affidavit, forged of course, and keep her dear daddy away from the office forever. She didn't know if that meant giving him something to take him out or keeping him sedated. All she knew was she wanted what was hers and, as greedy as she was, taking him out seemed to be an idea that popped into her mind a little too often.

Her next stop was Kory's house.

"Hey, I heard about your dad. How are you and your mom?" he asked.

She mustered up a few tears. "Not good. Can I come in?"

He hesitated, but he stepped aside. "Sure."

She stepped inside and sobbed for a moment or two, told him the details what happened, and ended with telling him her dad would be fine if he took it easy.

"Wow that is horrible. I must go and see him."

"Yes, but please, Kory, I didn't tell him about us. His heart can't take the truth. I told him you were in Chicago when he was in the hospital. Just please promise me you won't tell him about us. Please?" she begged.

"Are you serious right now? It's been weeks," he said looking at her like she was the coke-head she was.

"I know, Kory, and I wanted to tell them, I did. But I was so afraid, and had hopes we'd work it out. I didn't want to tell my parents we were done and then we worked it out."

"Tressa, you've gotta be kidding me. I mean, you went back to using drugs and you thought I'd take you back from that?"

"Again, I didn't go back to using, Kory. I hit it that night, yes, and I told you Stephen gave it to me and I had no plans to use it."

For a second he almost believed her, but he now knew the real Tressa.

"All I'm asking is for you to just not say anything until he is better. It will kill him, Kory, to know I messed up again. Please?"

"Okay, Tressa, I won't, but you know the wedding is supposed to take place in a few weeks."

"I know, Kory, and I live with this load every day. I just can't bring myself to tell them. They love you so much and think so highly of you. I just can't tell them, especially not now."

He shook his head. "Look, I will run up and get dressed and go with you to your folks' house to visit your dad, but you have to tell them the truth, Tressa."

"I will, Kory, okay. And whether you believe me or not, I'm clean. I only fucked with that shit that night because I had a lot of shit on my mind. I'm not a coke-head."

He gave her a look and proceeded to go up and dress. When he came back down, they drove out to her family's house. Kory sat with her dad for a couple hours and finally Tressa took him home. She cried and pleaded to stay and he gave in as she knew he would. They lay in his bed together and she got close to him. He stiffened at first, but put his arms around her and held her tight.

She went to sleep with a smile on her face.

The next day, Tressa left, but asked if she could come back. Kory told her that wouldn't be a good idea. She asked him to come by the house to visit with her father again and he said he would.

She went home to change and check on her dad. She gave him his meds, along with a mild sleeping aid, and when she was done getting ready, he was already sleeping. She left, headed for TiMax. Wallace was the first person on her list to see. She barged into his office without knocking. "I need your help!"

"Okay?" he said with curious eyes.

"Signed affidavit. I know you have something with my father's signature on it. I need an affidavit drawn up with the studio's heading and his signature so I can have proof of creative control around this place."

"They will never go for it, Tressa. You know they will contact your dad and our lawyers with the quickness."

"You need not worry about that. It's not for these idiots here at the studio. It's for Kory to see that I'm just as powerful and important as Tiffany is around here."

"Tressa, you're marrying the guy. Tiffany isn't a threat. Come on now, this could get me into a lot of trouble."

"And your ass can be fired by this afternoon. All I have to do is run and tell my daddy how you tried to take some pussy in this here office and your ass will be jobless. Get me the affidavit!" she yelled.

While she waited, Wallace went into his files and grabbed a memo from Mr. Green. He did a

few tricks and handed Tressa what looked like a
legal document.

"That wasn't so painful, was it? I'll remember
you when I eventually take over this company."
She slid the paper into her briefcase. "See you
around."

Next, she headed to Colby's. She had to make
sure he cut back on whatever he was doing and
got back to wooing Tiffany.

He tried to return the money and say he was
done, but of course she wasn't hearing that and
threatened to ruin his career. Coke-head or not,
she had a lot of clout in L.A. When she talked,
people listened. After he assured her he was on
the job and guaranteed he'd keep her away from
Kory, she left, headed for Kory's.

When she got there, she tried to reason with
him, but he refused to go through with the
wedding. She even swore she'd take a drug test.
When he told her that he wasn't going to change
his mind, she went for her briefcase and pulled
out her loaded gun: the fake affidavit.

"Okay, so your incoherent father has given you
control of the station. What does that bullshit
have to do with me?"

"Well, this means I can authorize shows or
shut down shows." She sat back in her chair to
give it a moment to sink in.

"Really, Reesy, still you're saying nothing."

"Let me be your Q-tip. *Boy Crazy* is supposed to premiere this fall. If you don't want to see your homegirl's show get shut down, you will meet me at the altar. All I want is one year, just one, Kory, and then you can walk."

"So if I go through with this marriage, you get your trust and you'll let Tiffany keep her show?"

"That's exactly what I'm saying. My father is not going to be down for long, Kory. Maybe he'll pick them back up in a year or two. But if you don't agree to marry me, I go to my afternoon meeting and pull the plug. And Tiffany's ass will be right back where she started when KCLN cancelled her corny-ass show!"

"You know what, Tressa, I thought you were the wicked bitch of the West, but I was wrong. You are worse, and right now, I can't think of a word low enough to say what I think of you."

"I'm sure that by the honeymoon you'll think of a word, but until then, do we have a deal?" When he didn't say anything after a few moments, she called his bluff. "Okay, no wedding, no show." She stood and walked toward the door.

"I'll do it!" he yelled after her.

She turned around with a big smile on her face. "One year, and it won't be so bad. I promise," she teased.

"I'm not doing this for you. Just so you know, I love Tiffany just that much to suffer with you for a year."

"I'm sure, but Colby is going to keep her occupied until we exchange vows." She smirked and headed for the door.

"You did pay him, didn't you?" he asked.

She turned to him. "Come again?" she asked with her head tilted to the right.

"Colby; you paid him to go out with Tiffany."

"I see you have been talking to my dear friend, Amber," she said. "She is definitely getting a sucky shower gift."

"Did you?"

"I did what I had to do, and if you breathe a word, I'll deny it and the show will go bye-bye. Now I'm sure I'll see you at the house around eight to visit with my dad."

She opened the door and walked out. Stepping off the porch, she heard a thud. It sounded like he had thrown something. Then she heard a muffled curse.

She got into her car smiling.

Chapter Twenty-nine

Tressa drove back to her parents' house feeling like forty-five million bucks, the amount of her inheritance. A year and some change was all she had to wait to finally have the money she was supposed to already be enjoying years ago, instead of still being on an allowance. She was so done with asking for an extra couple thousand here and there from her mom. All of her major purchases and splurges were made when she got a royalty check from her endorsements. She had a cosmetic line that she had run into the ground by spending more than she made. Her daddy had generously bought her out and gave her a share of the profits, but it still wasn't enough to maintain the luxurious lifestyle she wanted to have.

Her wedding was on her daddy, her condo was paid in full by her daddy, and she was on her third luxury car, also paid for by Daddy. She had wrecked her first two with her drinking and driving.

She knew she needed to go back into rehab if she wanted to kick her coke habit entirely, but she refused because she felt she finally had it under control. She didn't think she was anywhere close to how she had been a few years ago when she was dabbling in other drugs. Back then, she'd get so high that she couldn't function. Those days were gone. She could now snort a few lines and keep going as if she were clean. But she made sure she stayed away from Kory when she used, because he could tell she was different.

She would have never been busted that morning, if he hadn't been in her ear, whining like a baby about not getting any attention and time from her. She only went to his house to keep him out of her ear the next day. *What a big mistake that was,* she thought as she pulled up to her parents' gate. She wanted to check on her father, and Kory agreed to come by, so she wanted to freshen up and work on maybe making him want her beyond the year, because she did care for him—not love, but care—and she still wasn't going to let Tiffany win him over like she had won over her father.

"*Hola, mamá, como estas?*" She kissed her mother on the cheek.

"*No es bueno, bebé. Su padre es el amor de mi vida y tengo miedo,*" Tressa's mother cried, telling her it wasn't good. She told her daughter that Mr. Green was the love of her life and she was scared. "I don't know what I will do without your father," she said in broken English.

Tressa wrapped her arms around her momma and held her. "Shhhhhh, *mamá. No llores, papá va a estas bien*," she said, telling her mother that her dad would be just fine.

She stayed and comforted her mom before she went up to see her father. He was sitting up watching the news when she walked in.

"Hey, Daddy, how are you feeling?"

"Better. I was a little fatigued today. That medicine has me so drowsy. I need to talk to the doctor and ask him for something that doesn't make me so groggy." He looked great, something Tressa didn't want.

"We'll see, Daddy. For now, you need to just take it easy."

"I am, Isa, but you know me. I can't stay down for long. I've got to get back into the swing of things."

"Daddy, listen, work will be there when you are well enough to go back. Mommy's scared to death to lose you, so just relax. I can handle things, and I wish you'd trust me at TiMax. I'm far from being an idiot."

"I know you're not an idiot, Isa. I know that, but again, you're not ready. Your entire adult life has been a disappointment to your mother and me. I would have loved to give you a seat on the board, but your actions speak louder than your words."

"Daddy, for two years, I have been clean and sober, yet you still won't give me a chance," she cried.

"Just focus on getting married, Isa, and leave it alone. You are not fit to run my network, so just please, get married. Show me that you can be a responsible woman like your mother. After a year, you get your trust, and after that we will revisit this request to be a part of the network. But right now," he said tenderly, "the answer is still no."

She put her head down. "Why do you act like Tiffany Richardson is your prized possession and I'm not?" she asked sadly. "From the very first moment that you met her, Daddy, it's about her. You talk about how great she is and how she is this and how she is that. I'm your daughter, not her. Why do you act as if she is the apple of your eye, Daddy?"

"Isa, that isn't true at all. I will admit I admire that young lady's drive and creativity. She has never been in a tabloid, not to my knowledge, or in rehab, and when we did her drug test, she was clean. You bad-mouthed her, trying to convince me that she and Kory had a relationship and then I found out you lied, Isa. For what?

"She doesn't even care if you and Kory are together. You have everything, and yet you feel threatened. I found out she grew up without a father and I asked myself if my baby girl would be different if she hadn't had a wealthy father who spoiled the hell out of her. If my wife and I would have said no just some of the time, would she have not caused us so much grief and heart-ache? Would she not have brought shame to her family with the criminal charges for reckless behavior?

"When your mother and I brought you from the hospital, Isa, you were this little bundle of perfection. And then you grew up, and by fourteen, it was situation after situation, cir-cumstances after circumstances. And your poor mother, my Lord, Isa, she has cried her eyeballs out over you. I've held my wife, telling her that you'd get better. Up until maybe eigh-teen months ago, not quite two years, hardly anything has changed. Yes, you've brought it down a couple notches, but you've still been into trouble, Isabella. You wrecked a Bentley, and even though it was your fault, you still tried to blame someone else. You've been in more trouble than anyone we know. *TMZ* is a successful show just because of you, and you act as if you're oblivious when it comes to your behavior.

"Isa, I love you, baby girl. God knows you are in the center of my heart. And I wish I could say that I was proud of you, but I can't. Kory Banks is the best thing to have ever happened to you. Your mother and I didn't think he'd stick around this long, so you will make me proud on your wedding day. That is when I will feel some kind of pride. To know you have succeeded at something that Tressa Isabella Green didn't destroy, sabotage, or run off."

By then, Tressa was in tears. She knew every word that came out of her father's mouth was truth and it cut like a double-edged sword.

"I'm so sorry, Daddy. I know that I've been trouble for a long time, but I've changed and I am going to prove it to you. I am going to get my act together and be a good wife and may even give you grandchildren. I want you to be proud of me." She stood, got his medication, and poured some water into his glass. "Here take your meds, Daddy, and get some rest. Kory will be by later to visit with you."

She didn't give him the sedative because she wanted him to be up to talk to Kory. Although she didn't plan on being with Kory beyond a year, she now needed to try to make it work so her father could be proud of her for something.

She wouldn't let Kory walk away without giving her a child. She needed anything to win back her daddy's eyes and heart. Tiffany was smart, ambitious, and hardworking and all that blah, blah, blah, but she wasn't a Green, she didn't have Langley Green's blood running through her veins. She needed to taint the golden girl's good-girl image, and she knew just how she would do it. All she needed was opportunity.

She went downstairs and chatted with her momma before heading to Kory's. She knew he may not have been in a mood to see her, but she wanted to be close to him. She had hopes that he would hold her and comfort her pain away. When she got there, he wasn't home. That was a total disappointment, so she pulled out her cell phone and called Stephen. He had a soiree going on at his place, so she headed over to have fun with him.

A couple days later, her dad was up and ready to return to work. Although she thought it was too soon, she knew he wasn't going to take no for an answer. Kory was holding up his end of the bargain and had even allowed her to move back in after she had cornered him with threats of making Tiffany's life a living hell. She wanted to convince everyone that she and Kory were fine. More than anyone, she wanted to convince Tiffany.

In her head, as a reminder that she had what her nemesis wanted, she replayed the shocked look on Tiffany's face when she had told her that they were back together and the wedding was still on. She knew Tiffany was jealous. She couldn't wait until they were married, so she could show Tiffany to be the loser she really was. After that, she'd get clean and give her daddy a grandchild. That was something she was sure she would win her daddy over with. Tiffany wasn't going to have Kory or her father. Tressa was still determined to figure out a way to destroy her show.

Chapter Thirty

Living with Tressa and not talking to Tiffany was driving Kory insane. All he thought about morning, noon, and night was Tiffany. He was going out of his mind trying to figure out how to get out of marrying Tressa. When news made it to Tiffany that he and Tressa were back together, she had called him and he knew from her voice that he had lost her forever. "Is it true?" was all she said when he picked up the phone. He had paused, swallowed hard, and whispered, "Yes." He heard her sniffle and then the call ended. He tried calling her over and over, but she never once answered his calls.

He hated the position he was in, but he would do whatever it took to keep Tressa from pulling the plug on Tiffany's show. This was the only way he could keep Tressa under control, because she absolutely hated Tiffany. He just wanted to get the year he agreed to over with. He just hoped he'd make it without killing Tressa. He hated to just be in the same room with her.

He headed to Keith's house for dinner. He hadn't spent much time lately with his cousin because the wedding was approaching fast. He spent more time with his fake fiancée to keep up the façade of them being the happy couple. He hated pretending. He hated to look her dad in the eyes, knowing he didn't love or want to be with his daughter. At times, he felt Mr. Green could sense it.

One afternoon at lunch, when the women were in the kitchen, he asked Kory, "Are you getting cold feet, son?"

Kory replied, "No, sir, it's just coming quickly and I'm a li'l nervous."

His future father-in-law looked at him like he was searching for a true answer, so Kory said, "Mr. Green, I assure you, I'm not having second thoughts." Mr. Green smiled and offered his future son-in-law a glass of imported Scotch.

"So good to see you, cuz," Keith said when he opened the door. He gave him a brotherly hug.

"You too, man. It's like we always have something going on, and with the wedding approaching, I've been mad busy," he said.

"Speaking of this wedding, why in the hell are you going through with it? I mean, come on, Kory. It is obvious that you are in love with Tiffany. Tressa is not the one and you know it."

"True, and that is the only reason I am going through with this. You know Tressa's dad had that heart attack. Since then, Tressa's been running the network for him, and if I don't go through with this, she is going to shut Tiff's show down, cuz. I can't let that happen. All Tressa needs is a year to get her inheritance and then she and I can divorce. I love Tiffany, you know that. I'm doing this for her."

"You mean to tell me that she is threatening Tiffany's show if you don't meet her at the altar?"

"Yes, that's the gist of it."

"Damn, that's fucked up, but at least I know now that you're not a total idiot. And I hate that you have to endure this coke-head for a year for Tiffany's sake, but what other choice do you have? Tiffany would be devastated if her show was shut down after all the hard work she's put into it and all she's been through to keep it. I've visited her set a couple times, and she is on her business, cuz. But you love her that much to endure a year with this coke-head?"

"I love her that much and I'd suffer a decade for her if I had to," Kory said.

"Why don't you go to her, man? Just talk to her and tell her why you're going through with this.

Explain to her that you're only doing this to save her job and she will understand. Tiff will hear you out."

"I can't, cuz. If I do, it will cause problems for her. You know Tiff, man, she is a lioness. She isn't going to take that shit from Tressa. She will confront her about this and she'd beat the shit out of her and end up locked up."

"I know, li'l cuz, but damn. Tressa is a bitch on so many levels."

"I know, but I can deal with her as long as Tiffany is happy and successful and living out her dream. She works so hard. I just have to do what it takes to make sure she stays happy."

The doorbell rang and Keith excused himself to answer the door. Kory was shocked to see Tiffany and she looked just as shocked to see him.

They both looked at Keith. He held up his hands and said, "Y'all really need to talk," and quickly exited the room.

"I had no idea," Kory said.

"It's okay, Kory, it's fine." Tiffany took a seat on the opposite end of the sofa.

"How have you been? You look beautiful."

"I'm good, just working a lot. Work is pretty much the only fulfillment I'm getting out of life right now." She flashed him a quick smile.

"Really? Where is your superstar boyfriend?"

"Colby's been pretty busy working a lot lately too, so we haven't had much time together." She looked toward the door as if she was waiting for somebody.

"That's too bad," he said.

"Yes, but I guess that's how it goes. And you . . . I see this wedding is really going to happen." Kory saw her look past him again, as if she was watching for Keith.

"Yes." He paused from the Tressa subject. "Did you need something? You keep looking at the entryway."

"Actually, a glass of wine is what I need. I was looking out for Keith."

"Oh, I'll get it," he volunteered.

"Thanks, Kory," she said before he went through the door.

He came back and handed her a glass of red wine. "Here you go," he said.

She took a little sip and he went back to the other side of the couch. "So back to Tressa," she said. "How did she convince you to take the plunge with her? Is she back in rehab?"

"Well, she swears she's clean, so that's not it. I'm doing it for other reasons," he said, hesitating. He didn't want to lie to Tiffany, but he didn't want to tell her the truth either.

"Like?" she asked.

"Listen, Tiffany, don't worry about that, okay? After a year, she will have her inheritance and she'll be outta my hair."

She raised her brow. "Kory Lamar Banks, don't tell me that you are marrying that woman for her money?"

He frowned. "Hell no, Tiff. You know I'm not that guy. I couldn't care less about her money."

"Then what then, Kory? I'm not going to lie, okay? I spend every waking moment wondering how you can want to be with someone like Tressa. She is an addict, so why, Kory?" She looked sad.

"Tiff, I just have to, okay? But I want you to know that I wish it were you."

She swallowed hard and tears came to her eyes. "Kory, don't—"

"No, Tiffany, I've got to say this. I love you, and it's always been you. But for some reason, somehow, we can't seem to be at the same place at the same time. Trust, I don't want to marry Tressa. I can't stand the sight of that woman. If I didn't love you so much, I'd never speak to her ever again."

"Me? What do I have to do with your decision to marry that evil bitch, Kory? She hates me and she doesn't even try to hide it, so how are you doing this for me?"

"I didn't want to tell you, Tiff, but I have to. You have to know the truth about the situation with Tressa and me. Now that her dad has these health issues, she is basically filling his shoes. If I don't marry her for at least a year for her to get her inheritance, she is going to pull the plug on your show."

Tiffany burst into laughter. She wiped her eyes and cleared her throat. "What? Is that what she told you?"

Kory was confused. This wasn't the reaction he expected. "Yes, she brought over this document a couple weeks ago proving that she was now running the show."

"Kory, Tressa isn't running anything, as far as I know. Mr. Green has declared that she'll never work at his station. She is the joke of the studio and everyone, but you obviously, knows that." She polished off her wine and fiddled with the empty glass.

"So she's not in charge?"

"Not even in charge of the coffee girl." She handed him her glass.

"So she's been playing me? She gets up every morning, gets dressed, and tells me she is heading to the studio to work. She comes home in the evenings as if she's had an exhausting day. I've called her and she'd pick up and say she's in a meeting and she'll call me right back."

"I'm sorry, Kory. She's always there, but believe me, she doesn't work there." She touched his hand.

Kory looked at her and she looked at him, neither seeming to be able to turn away. He leaned in to kiss her and as soon as their lips touched, her cell phone rang. It was Colby.

"Please don't answer that," he said.

"I have to," she said.

"No, you don't." He grabbed the back of her head with his free hand and pushed his tongue into her mouth.

She dropped her cell phone on the floor and reached for his neck. He kissed her so deeply and passionately that she wanted more, but she stopped him.

"Kory, wait, wait. Wait please." He pulled back and looked into her eyes. "What do you want from me?" she asked.

"Your love, that's it. I don't love Tressa, Tiffany. I love you, and I am not going to allow her to manipulate me into marrying her. I know you are with Colby, Tiff, but I want you and I want you to be mine." She put her head down. He set her glass down and used two fingers to lift her chin. "Do you love him, Tiffany?"

"Yes," she said softly. His heart stopped and then she continued. "But not the way I love you."

Able to breathe again, he put his arms around her and squeezed her so tight. "I love you too, Tiffany, so much, and I want us to be together. Not just for a little while or a fling or date. I want you to be my wife."

Her eyes bulged. "Your wife?"

"Yes. I've held you in my heart for years, Tiffany, and I don't want to be with anyone else. I only want you. I've thought about it for a very long time and I know it's you."

"I know it's you too," she said and he kissed her again. "How are you going to handle Tressa?" she said, bringing him back to the subject.

"Play her game. She wants to play me for a fool, well, two can play that game."

"What are you going to do?"

"The last thing any woman would want to happen to them," he said.

After he told her his plans, he called Keith back down. The three of them ate and Kory and Tiffany decided to stay over to have some privacy, since Tressa was at Kory's and Colby could pop up whenever at Tiffany's.

Kory called Tressa and told her that he was going to stay over at Keith's and she didn't argue. Tiffany called Colby back and said she'd be with Asia. He went with that after she insisted that her friend needed her that night.

Chapter Thirty-one

Kory opened the guesthouse door and let Tiffany walk in first. He shut the door and grabbed her waist from behind and planted a couple soft kisses on her neck.

"Are you sure you're ready for this?" he asked.

She turned to him and smiled. "I've never been so sure about anything in my life, Kory. I've dreamed of making love to you so many times that I feel like I'm in a dream right now."

"Well, this isn't a dream, Tiffany, and I want to be the last man you give your body to. I want to be the last man you say 'I love you' to. I want to be the last man to kiss you good-bye in the mornings and I want to be the last and only man to make you happy."

"You can be that," she said.

"You are so beautiful, Tiffany, and through it all, you have held a place for me in your heart. I thank you for that." He gave her a gentle peck.

"It wasn't purposely done, Kory," she said and laughed a little. "It's just no matter who I was with or how I tried, I've never been able to get over you."

"Well, I thank God that you couldn't." He began to unbutton the buttons on her dress. When he got halfway done, he pushed the straps from her shoulder and her dress hit the floor. She pulled his shirt out of his jeans and he lifted it over his head and then removed his tank. She leaned in and planted soft kisses on his chest and he closed his eyes. She kissed him down to his stomach and undid his belt and jeans and he pushed them away and stepped out of them.

"Come here," she said and took his hand.

They went over to the bed and she took a seat and pulled him directly in front of her. His erection was huge. She took a deep breath and released it from his boxer briefs. The head sprang out and was pointed toward her mouth. She looked up at him.

"You don't have to," he said, hoping she would.

"I want to," she whispered softly. She kissed it before she received him inside of her mouth.

His legs and body quivered from the pleasure she gave him. She was more than good at it, he thought. She was the best. He hadn't had head like that in years.

"Tiff, baby, ahhhhh. Baby, that feels so damn good," he moaned.

She looked up at him as she continued to please his erection, bobbing her head up and down. She grabbed hold of the base, stuck her tongue out, and teased the tip.

Kory was more than ready to pleasure her. He pulled away, pulled her up, and pushed his tongue back inside her mouth as he pushed her panties down. She reached behind her back to unhook her bra, but he stopped her.

"No. Keep that on; it's so pretty on you." He gave her a little nudge and she lay back onto the bed.

He paused to admire her body and her sexy breasts sitting in the cups of her pretty satin blue bra before he climbed on top of her. He kissed her before making his way down to her neck and then he pulled her breasts out over her bra and licked and sucked her nipples hungrily. She moaned out loud.

He went for her clit and she spread her legs wider. To both of their surprises, she climaxed right away. She laughed at herself.

"You came that fast?" he asked, shocked.

"Yes, yes, yes." She continued to laugh.

"Why are you laughing?"

"Because I'm embarrassed."

"Why?"

"Because that was like forty seconds."

He laughed too. "Yeah, but now it's my turn, and trust me, baby, I'll be a lot longer than that." He moved back up to kiss her.

"I hope so," she said and pulled him close.

He slowly kissed her as he slid inside of her. She closed her eyes and moaned softly in his ear and he breathed deeply, enjoying her body. Being inside of Tiffany was exactly like he had imagined it would be. He pushed deeper and deeper and her moans grew louder and louder. He rose up, pushed her legs back, and looked at her breasts as they bounced with every stroke. He locked eyes with her and had to slow down. Just looking at her got him more excited and he wanted to explode. "What's wrong, Kory?" she asked.

"Nothing, I just want to enjoy you longer. I'm not ready to cum."

She reached for his hands and locked her fingers in his. She held his hands tightly and rolled her hips back on him. She pushed her pelvis into his and pushed when he pushed. She closed her eyes again and he just looked at her, thinking of how beautiful she was to him.

"Turn on your side," he whispered and pulled out.

She rolled onto her side and lifted her left leg to allow him access. Once he was in, she dropped her thigh and he pulled her body closer to his, grabbed a breast firmly, and began to stroke her again. She pressed her ass into him and that tingle came back, so he pulled out quickly.

He continued to massage her breast while he focused on pulling back from the eruption that was building in his dick.

"Let me back in," he said.

She lifted her leg again and he found his way back inside. He closed his eyes and they rocked the bed for a little while longer before she was on her stomach. He spread her cheeks and slid in and understood why that position was called the "cum snatcher." All it took was six or seven pumps and he couldn't hold it in any longer. He tried to, but it was over. He released it inside of her with a loud groan.

He came down and rested on her back for a brief moment and then he got up and lay beside her. She turned to him and smiled at him and he smiled back at her.

Then she frowned slightly. "Kory, why didn't we use a condom?"

"I didn't want to," he said.

"Were you using condoms with Tressa?"

"Yes," he said. Even if he didn't want to, his ex-fiancée had insisted. "However, I haven't been with Tressa sexually since before I broke off our engagement. Were you using condoms with Colby?"

"Yes." He believed her.

"Listen, Tiff, maybe that was a stupid move, but you are different. It's like I've known you my entire life, and, I don't know, I feel safe with you. I mean after I went off to school, I moved on from my high school fantasy to be with you, but I never forgot you. You were always lingering in the back of my mind, and you are it. You are my match."

"I feel safe with you too, Kory, and my world is perfect right now at this very moment." She moved into his arms.

"So you think you can handle keeping your distance from Colby until after the wedding?" he said.

"Yeah, I can avoid him. It's a little less than two weeks, so I can avoid him and try to keep my cool around Tressa. You know I want to punch her in her face."

"I know, babe, but Tressa is going to get what she deserves in due time, so don't even sweat her. Just keep your cool, and in a couple weeks, this will all be over. Just keep our thing quiet until then. I don't want to tip her off."

"I will, but it's just going to be hard to keep you a secret," she said, locking her fingers into his again. "I want to shout it to the world that I'm finally with the love of my life."

"I know, babe, soon. We just have to do this the right way. Your show is the root of everything and I don't want to jeopardize it."

"I know," she said and he kissed her forehead.

They went another round and then crept into the main house for another bottle of Merlot. They sat up and talked all night and didn't fall asleep until the sun was coming up the next morning.

Chapter Thirty-two

When Tiffany finally made it to the studio the next day, she was glowing. All she thought of was Kory, and when Colby called, she didn't answer. She sent him a text saying she was swamped with work, and when he asked could he come over that night, she told him she was too tired and just wanted to rest.

She packed an overnight bag and met Kory at Keith's again, and the second they closed the guesthouse door, they were snatching away their clothes. They made love as if they hadn't the night before. The next morning, she had to literally force herself to leave his side. It took her ten minutes to get into her car. As soon as she exited the gates of Keith's estate, Kory called her phone and they talked her entire ride to work. When she got to the studio, she went to her office for a minute before heading to the set.

She walked in to find Myah smiling at her. "Good morning, Myah," she said. "I see I'm not the only one smiling today."

"Well, I'm smiling because I want to know the dirt," Myah said.

"What dirt?"

"Come on, Tiff, you have been floating for two days, and this morning when I got in, there was a delivery guy here with flowers for you." She followed Tiffany into her office. On her desk was a gigantic bouquet of roses. It looked like it was about five dozen in all.

"Myah, you know Colby sends me flowers all the time," she said, going for the card. She stopped to take a sniff of the fragrant arrangement.

Myah's eyebrows rose. "Yes, but the last time I checked, Colby's initials were CG, that card said they are from KB."

Tiffany smiled. She had to tell somebody, because she was bursting. She had only told her girls Rose and Asia.

"Okay, okay, okay," she said. She went to shut her office door. "I'm going to tell you, Myah, but you have to promise me that you won't say a word."

"I promise," Myah said.

"Mee-Mee, I'm serious, not one word to anyone. And you know if you tell Dee, all of L.A. will know."

"Okay I promise, Tiff. Now who is the mystery man?

"It's Kory," Tiffany said. A bright smile formed on her face.

"As in Kory Banks, fiancé of the boss's daughter?" Myah looked shocked.

"Yes," Tiffany squealed.

"Hold on, I thought you said you didn't love him anymore."

"I lied, okay? And the other night, we got together and talked, and turns out the only reason he was going to marry Tressa was for me."

"Wait a minute, now I'm really confused."

"Okay, listen, I gotta give you the really short version. Tressa had him believing she had the power to shut down *Boy Crazy* if he didn't marry her. She has been pretending to be acting CEO since Mr. Green had his heart attack and she told Kory he'd have to marry her for a year for her to get her inheritance and for me to keep the show. Now, I must get to the set, but please, Myah, don't repeat this, because Kory and I have a plan to get back at her."

"What? What is it?"

"I can't tell you right now, Myah, but this is our secret."

"My lips are sealed," she said.

Tiffany hurried out to the set.

***

Kory sat on a stool in the kitchen and tried to read his paper and drink his orange juice, but all he could think of was Tiffany. He couldn't wait until the day ended so he could see her again. He knew he didn't owe Tressa anything, but he had been gone the last two nights, and even though they were not having sex, he didn't want her to be suspicious.

"I'm off to work," Tressa said, coming into the kitchen dressed to kill in another tailor-made business suit.

He decided to fuck with her. "Already?" he asked, looking at his watch.

"What do you care?" she asked and opened the cabinet for her thermal coffee cup.

"You know what, Tressa, I don't, but I guess since we have to appear to be the happy couple, we need to start acting like one."

"Go on," she said, stopping to hear him out.

"I was thinking, since you're the big CEO, I should drop in and bring you lunch and let you take me around for a tour, you know. I send you flowers and all like a good fiancé; maybe if I showed my face, people would believe that we really are good."

"Kory, that's not necessary. Plus, I have back-to-back meetings today, so you don't have to do that." She reached for the coffee.

"But I want to. I mean, I don't hate you, Tressa, and we will be married in a couple weeks. A year is a long time to live with someone and not get along, so we should make the best of it."

"Where is this coming from?"

"Listen, Reesy, a few weeks ago, I was planning to marry you for real. I loved you and part of me still does. So, since I have to be in this for a year, I don't want to be miserable."

"I see," she said and looked at him closely.

"So what do you say I come and take you to lunch today?" he suggested.

"Okay, you can take me to lunch, but no tours and meeting folks. I don't have time for that," she said going for the front door.

"I bet you don't," he said under his breath.

"Huh? What was that?" she yelled back into the kitchen.

"Nothing, I'll be there around one," he said and she left.

He went by the jewelry store, and every free moment, he was texting Tiffany. He called her and told her about picking Tressa up for lunch and she said she'd make sure she'd be in the building so she could run into him.

Tressa went into her dad's office and told his assistant she was expecting Kory to take her to lunch and to just alert her when he was there.

When his assistant asked her what she needed in Mr. Green's office, she made up something about adding a couple of new photos to his desk. Five minutes after she got there, her dad's assistant buzzed the office to let her know Kory was there. She came out with her purse as if she had been there all morning. As soon as they got to the bottom floor, the elevator doors opened to find Tiffany waiting to go up.

"Tressa, Kory, what a surprise," she said.

"Why would it surprise you? This is my dad's company," Tressa said.

"I know, but running into you is so rare around here," Tiffany returned.

"That's because you're on your set all day, putting together an awesome show, I assume."

Tiffany smiled and held in her laugh. "Yep, that is exactly what I've been doing."

"I'm sure you will do well," Kory said.

"I hope so, Kory, I'd hate to see my show shut down."

"I'm sure you're good. Tressa knows how great your show is. And she'd be a fool to let go of the hottest show TiMax has ever seen. Plus, we will be married soon, so television will not exist in our house for at least a year, right, sweetheart?" Kory pulled Tressa close.

"You're so right," Tressa said. "We'll be too busy doing what newlyweds do. Next year about this time, we may have a little one, who knows."

"On that note, I'll get up to my office. Again, Kory, congrats, you picked a winner." She winked and stepped onto the elevator when the doors opened again.

"I'll see you around," Kory said as the doors closed.

"I thought you said you and Tiffany were no longer friends," Tressa barked.

"Yes, that is true. We are no longer friends."

"So what's with the 'see you around'?" she asked, a hand on her hip and an eyebrow raised.

"It's an expression, Reesy, relax," he said and they walked out the building. "Where do you want to go for lunch?"

"Someplace fancy, I want to show you off," she said as he opened the car door for her.

When they got to the restaurant, a couple of regulars recognized Tressa. She proudly confirmed that they'd be attending her wedding, while Kory secretly laughed on the inside. Little did she know that was going to be the most embarrassing day of her royal life. He hoped everyone who was anyone would attend; he just prayed it didn't backfire, because Tiffany's show was at stake. He hoped she was right when she said spoiled little Tressa had no power, because he was ready to pay her back for all the drama she had caused for him and Tiffany.

Chapter Thirty-three

"What are you thinking about?" Tiffany asked Kory.

"Tomorrow," he answered.

"What about tomorrow, baby?" she asked concerned, because this was the last night they would have to hide their relationship.

She had waited until that evening to break up with Colby and he kept asking her why. The only thing she could say to keep him from calling Tressa was she was just no longer interested. It was apparently hard for him to believe and accept, because he kept calling and texting every five minutes, so she had to power off her phone when Kory arrived.

"Am I doing the right thing, Tiff? I mean, what if Mr. Green decides to pull the plug on your show? I'm sure he is going to be pissed after everything goes down tomorrow."

"Listen, my love, the show has recorded damn near twelve episodes. In two weeks, we have a live interview on TiMax with the entire cast. He is not going to throw millions of dollars out the window. The contract gives us two seasons, whether it's a hit or a miss, so I will be employed for at least that amount of time. After, if not, I'll just have to sell my house, move in with you, and you can support me for the rest of my life," she said and kissed him.

"I plan to do that anyway," he said and sat up. "I just know how hard you've worked, Tiff."

"Kory, nothing on this planet is worth more than us. If tomorrow causes me to lose the show, it doesn't matter anymore. As long as I got you, I am more than okay." She gave him a bright smile.

"I love you, Tiffany, and I am proud of you for being such a fighter. You inspire me to love harder and work harder, and I know deep down inside that you are my future."

"I know, Kory, and I love you too," she said and kissed him. "Now you have a bachelor party to get back to before they realize you're missing." She handed him his boxers.

"Do I have to go back?"

"Yes, Keith went through a lot to get the top strippers in L.A.; you can't miss out on that."

"You're right, it's hard to find quality strippers," he said. He got up to get dressed.

Tiffany walked him to the door and hugged his neck super tight and gave him a final kiss. "I love you," she yelled before he got into his car.

"I love you too. And be on time tomorrow. It won't work if you're not there."

"Baby, I'm there!" she called out. She went into her room and got into the bed. Before she turned out the lamp, she noticed a little tent card on the nightstand. She picked it up and opened it.

> *You are cordially invited to the fake wedding of the century. Bring your sexiness along with an overnight bag, because our honeymoon is paid in full.*
> *I love you, Tiffany.*
> *Kory*

Tiffany hopped out of her bed and made a dash to her closet. She didn't know how many days they'd be gone, but she was going anyway. She would put Darryl in charge while she was gone. She packed all the things she thought were essential and then she got into bed and grabbed her cell phone and powered it back on. She texted Kory and when he replied, she laughed. He had sent her a picture of one of the strippers bent over in front of him and typed, I wish this was your ass in my face. She replied, telling him to have fun but behave and to call her when he was on the way home.

A couple hours later he called and she hopped up like a rabbit to take his call. They talked his entire drive home. When he got in, they got off long enough for him to shower and then stayed on the phone until they both fell asleep. The next morning, both of their phones were still running because they had never pressed the END call button.

Chapter Thirty-four

"Mr. Green, you're here early," Kory said, surprised to see him.

"Yes, the girls sorta kicked me out of my house. It's like a circus, with makeup, hair extensions, and you name it."

"I bet." Kory tried not to give Mr. Green eye contact. He was starting to have second thoughts about his plans to dump Tressa at the altar, but it wasn't about Mr. Green. It was about him, Tressa, and Tiffany. Tressa had drawn first blood, and he wanted to let the world know what kind of a person she really was.

"Listen, son," Mr. Green said. "I know today is a big day for you two, and my wife and I wanted to give you a little something. Tressa can be a handful, and until she gets her trust, she is going to want to keep up the lifestyle she's lived." He handed Kory a certified check for $2 million.

Kory couldn't believe his eyes. "Sir, no, I can't take this. I mean, this is about how much

I have to my name, and I'm sure she won't run through it in a year."

"Trust me, son, take it. This is our gift to you and your new bride."

"Look, Mr. Green, I know where you, as her father, are coming from. You can give this to Tressa if you want her to have it, but as a man, I can't accept this. Tressa knows who she is marrying, and if what I have isn't enough, she picked the wrong man."

"I understand, Kory, and I respect you for being the man you are. I just know my Isabella and I know we have spoiled her beyond the definition of spoiled, and I just don't want her to bring you down because of what her mother and I have done."

"Trust, sir, you have absolutely nothing to worry about," Kory said.

"Okay, but I will hold on to this, and if at any time you need it, it's yours." Mr. Green put the check inside his jacket pocket.

"Mr. Green, can I ask you one more thing? It's about Tiffany Richardson."

"Yes, I understand you guys go way back. High school, right?"

"Yes, sir, I just have to ask."

"What is it, son?"

"I need your word that no matter what happens with me and Tressa, you will never let our mess interfere with her position at TiMax."

"Listen, Kory, I am a wise man. Although I don't look like it, I am. I will never let my personal life cloud my business. Tiffany is smart, bright, and has a hit show on her hands. Her position at TiMax has absolutely nothing to do with my daughter. As long as she is doing a phenomenal job like she has been, she and her show have a home at TiMax."

"Thank you, sir, because your daughter led me to believe otherwise."

"Well, son, you're not the only one she's led to believe something that's far from the truth." He turned to walk out, but turned back. "One more thing, Kory," he said. "Do what's in your heart, son. Tressa will always land on her feet as long as she has me and her mother. She isn't the ideal daughter, but she is still my daughter. And as much pain and heartache she has caused and may continue to cause, I am going to always love and take care of my baby. Tressa will be fine no matter what you choose to do."

Kory gave him a faint smile. He could tell that Mr. Green knew Tiffany meant more to him than just a friend. "Are you sure, sir?" he asked, making sure he and Mr. Green was on the same page.

"Absolutely," he said. He winked at Kory and exited the room.

Kory grabbed his phone and texted Tiffany:

Game on! I love you!

The church was packed. Kory didn't leave the bishop's office until he got a text from Tiffany saying she was there. He told Keith he was ready and Keith went out and told Amber to start. Keith and Kory took their positions, and Kory scanned the church and tried to spot Tiffany. He saw her when she stood and then sat back down. He smiled.

After what seemed like hours, Tressa was finally coming down the aisle. She had a smile on her face and Kory smiled back at her.

He wondered if he should abort the plan, but he looked at the love of his life, sitting there counting on him to come through for her, and he knew that was what he had to do.

"Will you all be seated," the bishop said. "Who gives this woman away?" he asked. Tressa's parents stood and answered, "We do," and sat back down.

The ceremony continued and the bishop addressed Tressa first. She quickly said, "I will," and then he turned to Kory.

After he recited the vows, he just stood there.

her. She paced back and forward, fuming, daring anyone to approach her. Her father sat with her mother, attempting to comfort her.

Tressa ranted and raved for hours after everyone was gone and wouldn't leave the church. Her dad sent her mom home, while he stayed to take care of Tressa. After trying to convince her to come home for what seemed like forever, he said the only words she had been longing to hear him say: "Tressa, you can have your trust."

It helped to soothe the embarrassment and pain, but she knew she had to get Tiffany back for the humiliation that she and Kory had subjected her to.

She laid her head on her daddy's chest and cried harder than she had ever cried in her life.

Chapter Thirty-five

When Tiffany and Kory got back from their seven-day vacation, Tiffany had orders to see Mr. Green. She walked to his office nervously, prepared for her termination. She didn't care anymore at that point, because she and Kory were now engaged. He had proposed on the plane before they took off. They planned to have a wedding in Chicago in six months, so she didn't care what TiMax did to her.

"You wanted to see me?" she asked and she entered his office.

"Yes, come on in," he said. She came in and sat down. "That was quite a scene at the church," he said.

She put her head down. "I know, Mr. Green, and I had no idea that it would turn into a huge fiasco. I know it's childish, but Tressa has a side to her that you don't know. She's been horrible to me and Kory. I know Kory should have handled it another way, but your daughter has a way of bringing out the worst in people."

"Listen, Tiffany, that is personal business. I called you in my office just to tell you that you still have a home here at TiMax. What happened to my daughter was foul, but she deserved it. She put herself in that situation and she had to get a dose of her own medicine."

"You mean, I'm not fired?" Tiffany asked.

"No, but I expect your show to kick ass. And next week, I want you to be a part of the live interview with the cast."

"Mr. Green, that's not necessary. I'm more of a behind-the-scenes type."

"I insist. You are beautiful and talented, and you need to share your motivation with the viewers. Trust, it will be a benefit to the show if you come on and talk about what motivates you to create such a brilliant show."

"Thank you, Mr. Green. I will be ready," she said standing. "Is there anything else?"

"Yes, congratulations," he added.

"For what?"

"Your engagement." He gestured toward her hand. "Your finger didn't house that diamond a week ago."

"I'm really sorry, Mr. Green, for everything."

"No apologies. I told Kory to follow his heart. I know love when I see it, and the way he looks at you . . . He's never looked at my daughter like that, so congrats."

Tiffany smiled. "Thanks, Mr. Green."

She hurried back to her office. There, she grabbed the vodka and had two shots to calm her nerves. She wasn't fired and she couldn't wait to get home to tell Kory.

She sat down at her desk and her phone rang. It was Colby. She thought the scene at the church was the nail in the coffin, but that didn't stop him from calling every hour. She hit IGNORE again and finished her drink. She called Kory, but he didn't pick up, so she decided she'd go to the set and see what the latest was. After four more long hours, she headed to Kory's, where she planned to be for the rest of her life.

She went into the kitchen where he was cooking and gave him a kiss. "Hey," she said.

"Hey, how was your return to work?"

"Well, as you can see, I'm not fired, thank God. And next week, your fiancée is going to be on television."

"No way, seriously?"

"Yep, the exclusive interview with the cast of *Boy Crazy* will be on live on TiMax and Mr. Green said that he wants me to be on too."

"Babe, that is fantastic." He poured her a glass of wine. "I am so proud of you, Tiffany," he said and she smiled. "I told you that everything would be okay."

"I know, but I still hate it for Tressa, you know. Rumor has it her dad gave her the trust. I guess Mr. Green just wants her to be happy."

Kory took plates from the cabinet, so they could eat. "Well, I know Tressa well enough to know that the money isn't going to make her happy. She has issues, Tiff, and if she doesn't get herself together, she is going to self-destruct."

"Well, that's not your problem anymore, my love," she said and sipped. "Did Mr. Green tell you the damage for the wedding cost?" she asked as he fixed their plates.

"Well, surprisingly, he said I don't owe him anything."

"You're kidding, right? I mean, I didn't even see the reception hall, but I could tell that wedding put a dent in his wallet."

"Baby, this is Mr. Green we are talking about. The man is worth billions. He's run his network over thirty years. He isn't stressing about this. This is like nothing for him. Hell he is worth more than Oprah."

"True, but I still feel a little bad," she said.

"Me too, but it is what it is," he said and set her plate in front of her.

They ate and then they went out to sit on the patio and tried to enjoy each other, but every five minutes, Tiffany's phone rang. It was Colby. She didn't understand why he wouldn't stop calling her.

"Give me the phone," Kory said.

Tiffany hesitated. "Kory, come on, babe," she said. "I don't want you in the middle of this."

"Tiff, give me the phone," he demanded. She handed it over. "Hello," he answered. After listening, he said, "Listen, bro, this has got to stop. Tiffany has told you that it's over and done, so with all due respect, stop calling my woman's phone." He hung up.

"Kory, babe, I wish you hadn't done that," she said.

"Why, Tiff, because he heard you the last ten times you've told him to stop calling?"

"No, because I need to handle my own business. I don't need you to do that for me."

"Listen, I know you've been this strong, independent sister, doing it all for yourself for a long time. But I'm here now, and there is no more doing it for yourself. I am all in. I know you can fight your own battles, but you don't have to. I am here now, Tiffany. And you know we were raised in the same arena, and under the business suits is the same old hood Kory you knew in high school. Colby is going to have to stop calling your phone."

"Okay," she said and lay back into his arms. As strong as she wanted to be, she knew he was right. Colby was on her nerves and if it took Kory to check him to keep him from calling, she was all for that.

Chapter Thirty-six

Tiffany was in makeup getting ready for her television interview. Kory was there too. She had put her phone on silent because Colby was relentless and wouldn't stop calling and texting her. He begged her to talk to him, but she refused and didn't understand what was so urgent that he couldn't say in a voice mail or text. She smiled at Kory in the mirror as he watched as the makeup artist enhanced her face. She had butterflies flying around in her stomach, because she had never been interviewed on a live show before. She had done brief interviews on the red carpet and a couple articles here and there, but this was her first sit-down, "get into my head" interview. She hoped she wouldn't say anything goofy or hood. Her momma subscribed to TiMax that week just so she could watch and DVR it.

"How you feeling?" Kory asked.

"Nervous. Scared. I mean, I'm used to being *behind* the camera, Kory. What if I say the wrong thing?"

"Tiff, calm down, babe, you will do fine. You are gorgeous and all you have to do is go out there and answer the man's questions. And before you know it, it will be over and we will be heading home to a nice Bordeaux, soft music, and me." He kissed her hand.

"On that note," she said, "let's get this interview over with." The makeup girl removed the cape from around her neck and she stood. She took a couple deep breaths and gave Kory another smile.

"You are gorgeous and you are gonna be fine," he said.

"I hope so."

"In five, Miss Richardson," one of the crewmen said.

"I guess this is it," she said and headed toward the stage. She was shaking like a leaf.

"Okay, everyone, we have had a chance to talk to the crew and the newcomers of *Boy Crazy*," the host said. "Now it's time to meet the woman who makes it all happen. This show was created by a gentleman by the name of William Keiffer. It was a great concept, but when executive producer Tiffany Richardson joined the team, the show skyrocketed from number six to number one in just one season, and she is here to tell us how. Miss Tiffany Richardson," he said. She stepped onto the stage, took a seat, and the interview got underway.

She brought them up to date on how she got her position by chance and how it just all fell into place. She told them about her determination to keep the show going and how she just so happened to run into an old high school crush, who was engaged at the time to Mr. Green's daughter. "I met him, pitched the show, and here we are," she said with a smile.

"Wow, I can say you've done well for yourself," the host said. "And you know we have to address the drama, too."

"Listen, my fiancé and I hate how horribly things went, but we are past all of that now. I am looking forward to a phenomenal season, and the cast is going to blow viewers' minds."

"Well, I've had a chance to sit in on a few recordings, so I agree," he said with a smile. "We are going to take a peep at another clip from the show then bring the cast members back out and tell you guys about some of the guest stars who will be appearing on *Boy Crazy* this season."

They went to commercial and Tiffany blew out a breath, glad that her segment was over. The crew rushed out with more seating and the crew members took their seats. Tiffany stood, but the host told her that she was still on, so she sat back on the sofa.

The cameraman did a countdown and they were back. "We are back live with the cast of TiMax's very own new show, *Boy Crazy*," the host said.

They discussed the guest stars and show times and when the first episode would debut.

The host gave the final comments. "Before our show comes to an end, we want to congratulate everyone on the show. We know it was a battle, but *Boy Crazy* lives on. We have one final clip for you guys."

When the last clip began to play, Tiffany's heart dropped. It was her on stage, at the club on a pole.

"Oh my God, turn it off!" she yelled, thanking God her mic was off. But it kept playing; whoever was in the control room would not turn it off. The clip played through and she was in tears by the end and her heart was pounding. She snatched the mic off and ran to the control room. She wrenched the door open and found Tressa's evil ass. "What the hell is going on?"

Tressa sneered. "Tiffany one, Tressa two."

"Where did you get this?" Tiffany yelled.

"Your boyfriend, or should I say your whore? All I had to do was dangle a few dollars at him and he got with you, fucked you, used you, and played you," Tressa said getting in Tiffany's face.

Tiffany pushed her hard as she could. "Get the fuck outta my face!" she yelled.

"You bitch," Tressa said and pushed her back.

Kory came in and broke them up. He pulled Tiffany out of the control room and they hurried back to the set.

"Austin, what the hell was that!" Tiffany yelled at the host. "How did you let something like this happen?"

A million and one apologies came at her. "Tiffany, I had no idea that was going to happen," he said.

Tiffany was frantic, embarrassed. She knew now that Colby was a joke and the joke was on her. "I wanna go home," she cried. "Kory, take me home!"

Kory grabbed her by the hand and rushed her out of the studio.

Mr. Green rushed into the studio. "What the hell is going on?" he yelled. Everybody started looking around at each other. "Somebody explain this instant!" he yelled. Tressa walked out of the control room with the evidence in her hand. "What did you do?" he demanded.

"She humiliated me, Daddy," she cried.

"Isabella, what in the hell is wrong with you? You brought your personal issues to my studio. You brought your drama to my studio!"

"That bitch ruined my life. She took everything from me, including you!" she yelled.

Mr. Green looked at her, his jaw flaring. "Security," he called. "Please escort Miss Green out and make sure she leaves the premises."

"Daddy, you're going to throw me out?" Tressa cried when security rushed toward her. "Don't touch me, you bastard!" she told the one who reached for her. The guard looked at Mr. Green.

"Isabella, I love you, baby, but I'm done. I've given you all but my soul, and I am not going to contribute to your self-destruction anymore. You have caused our family too much heartache, pain, and embarrassment, so I'm done. You can have your beachfront condo and your Benz, but you will not get your inheritance or another dime from me. If you ever have children, they will be entitled to their portion, but as for you, you are now cut off. Now get the hell out of my studio."

The security guards moved toward Tressa again.

"No, please, Daddy!" she shrieked. "No, please no. Take your hands off me. Daddy!"

She sobbed. "No, Daddy, don't do this," she cried as they dragged her out.

Mr. Green watched as his only child was ejected from the building kicking and screaming. He turned and looked at Austin, the host of the show.

"I'm sorry, sir, I had no idea," Austin said.

"It's not your fault, Austin. Whoever let her in that control room and played that footage must be fired at once."

Mr. Green headed back to his office. He went straight for his Scotch and took a couple gulps. Then he pulled out his cell phone and called Tiffany, but she didn't pick up. He left her a voice mail. "Listen, Tiffany, I am so sorry, and whatever we can do for you, don't hesitate. Please know that I speak for myself and everyone here when I say that we never wanted something like this to happen. Please call me."

Chapter Thirty-seven

When they got to Kory's house, Tiffany was a mess. She had never been so humiliated in her life. Her phone was ringing off the hook and she wondered how long it would take for this to die down. She was afraid to show her face.

"I should have listened to you when you told me the truth about Colby," she said and took a swallow of her vodka. Wine wasn't going to cut it that time.

"Baby, shhhhh," Kory said, holding her tight.

"I should have. Now the whole world has seen my ass cheeks dancing on a pole. My mother has called fifty times, Kory," she cried. "How am I going to show my face in public?"

"Baby, it wasn't that bad, to be honest. You looked damn good for one, and TiMax is known for stuff like that, so it may do more good than harm."

She stared at him. "Kory, do you hear yourself? A clip of me pole dancing has aired on God knows how many televisions tonight. How is that a good thing?"

"Well, for one, you couldn't really tell it was you; the camera wasn't on your face. It barely focused in on your face, Tiff, until the end and they shut it off."

She felt like she was in the Twilight zone. "Kory, everybody who knows me knows that was me. Do you see my phone lighting up like a damn Christmas tree?"

Her phone vibrated again and she looked at it. When she saw Asia's number, she picked up. "Hello," she said impatiently.

"Oh my goodness gracious, gal, you didn't tell me that you were going to play a stripper on your own show. Girl, you were fierce. You need to teach me those moves."

"Asia, that wasn't a clip from the show. It was a scene from a dance I did for Colby's punk ass that I had no idea he recorded."

"Really? You looked so professional. I thought it was a scene from an upcoming show."

"Well, I had a few lessons, but it wasn't a scene, and I'm mortified."

"Well, I don't see why. Have you checked your Facebook and Twitter?"

"No, why?"

"Well everyone is talking about it and they all seem to love it. Here, I'll read some of it to you. Listen to this," she said. "'Do it, Tiff.' 'Girl, you are too sexy.' 'Now that's hot.'" Tiffany started to calm down. "Girl," Asia said, "no one knows that that wasn't part of the show."

"Get out," Tiffany said.

"Girl, I think you just boosted your ratings."

Tiffany got off the phone and told Kory to follow her. They went to the room and powered on her iPad. She started reading her comments and the Tweets. She saw that it wasn't so bad, because people really thought it was part of the show.

"Well, I'll be damned," she said. "How do people not get that this is real?"

"Count your blessings, love," Kory said and hugged her.

"I still want to give Colby a piece of my mind," she said and took another sip.

"Hey, look at me. Tressa, Colby, and the rest of that drama is all behind us. Block his number and we move on."

"You sure? Because I really, really wanna give him a Chi-Town beat down," she said.

He kissed her. "Me too, Tiff, but what would that solve or change?"

"Okay, you're right," she said and gave him a smile. Her phone rang again. It was her mother. "Let me take this. Hi, Ma," she said when she answered.

"Child, why didn't you tell Momma you were going to be shaking your ass on a pole? All my church friends were here to watch you on television."

"Momma, I'm sorry. I didn't know that clip was going to air tonight. It was actually edited out of the show," she lied. "I only did that to help one of the actors from the show."

"Well, it wasn't so bad, because I couldn't tell it was you at first, but I caught your face right before the clip ended. Betty Jean was the bigmouth who said, 'Ain't that Tiff?' and after that, they rewound the thing five times to make sure it was you."

"Momma, I'm sorry."

"It's okay, sugar. What's done is done."

"Listen, Momma, my line is burning up; can I call you tomorrow?"

They got off and she hung up. Relieved to have spoken to her mom, she didn't feel so bad. The next day, she found the courage to go to work. She made the trek to her office in the midst of unwanted applause. After she made it into her office, Mr. Green knocked on her door.

"Come in," she yelled.

"Tiffany, I can't begin to tell you how sorry I am for what happened."

"It's okay, Mr. Green, I'll survive. Word on the street is I was hot," she said with a smile.

"I know it turned out well, but this is something this network is responsible for. It's fortunate that it didn't get any negative backlash. Again, I'm sorry. And this is for any embarrassment or humiliation the station may have caused you. Please accept this as a token of apology." He put an envelope on her desk.

"Mr. Green, this isn't necessary," she said, not taking the envelope. "I'm fine."

"I insist. I have to share my wealth with someone," he said sadly.

"Mr. Green, I heard about you and Tressa. I'm really sorry," she said sincerely. She wished she had a dad like him in her life. Tressa didn't truly know what she had.

"Don't be. I just pray that this will be the wakeup call that Isabella needs to get herself together." He smiled. "Enjoy the rest of your day, Tiffany, and if you ever need anything, just ask; no hesitation."

"Thank you, Mr. Green," she said and he made his exit.

She stared at the envelope and wondered what Mr. Green had given her for her embarrassing moment on live television. She dropped the check on the desk when she saw the amount. Then she grabbed it and raced out of her office to catch up with him. "Mr. Green, Mr. Green," she called out as she caught up with him. "This must be some kinda mistake. I mean, last night was bad, but not forty-five million dollars bad."

"It's not a mistake, Tiffany, and if you don't want it, you can endorse it to charity. It's yours and I refuse to take it back. That money has been sitting and waiting to be spent by someone who deserves to have it, and I think that someone is you. Please do an old man a favor and accept."

"But, Mr. Green, this is—"

"Tiffany, I won't take it back," he said firmly.

"Well, I guess I'll just have to say thank you," she said with her heart racing.

She had a few hundred thousand, but millions? No, not her. Kory did, but not her. She told Myah she was taking a day and went to the jewelry store.

"Is he here?" she asked the clerk that was out front.

"Yes, he is," he said and let her back. She went to his office door and tapped.

"Come in," Kory yelled. When she opened the door, she saw he was on the phone. She shut the door softly behind her and came around and sat on his desk in front of him and started to unbutton her top slowly. She revealed her cute black and pink lace bra. Then she stood, hiked up her skirt, and removed her panties.

She could see Kory was struggling to concentrate on his conversation. She could see his dick began to swell.

"Hal, listen something just came up," he finally said. "Please let me call you right back." He hung up so fast Tiffany doubted the other person had time to agree.

As soon as he put the phone down, he went straight for her breasts. He pulled them out over her bra like he liked them and sucked them hungrily. She reached for his tie and began to pull it loose. Then she reached for his belt and undid his slacks. Within moments, he was inside of her. He pushed her legs back, opening them wider, and she heard her skirt rip. She began to moan louder. He leaned down and pushed his tongue into her mouth.

"I love you, baby, I love you," he panted as he licked her down her neck and went back to her left nipple. He sucked harder and stiffened. "Ahhhhh, baby. Aaaaahhhhhh." She smiled and kissed his nose.

"That was good, baby," she said.

He got up slowly. "Yes, it was." He pulled his boxers and pants up. "It's not even noon and you're here taking off your clothes in my office, what gives?"

She sat up, put her breasts back into the cups, and stood. She looked at the papers they'd crumpled and messed up on his desk. "First, I hope those papers wasn't important." She picked up her panties and stuffed them into her purse, adjusted her ripped skirt, and began to button her blouse.

"No, I can reprint them. Again, what brings you by, gorgeous? I know you have plenty of fan mail this morning."

"Yes, but that's not why I'm here. I got a gift this morning from Mr. Green."

He arched one eyebrow. "Okay, what was it?"

"A check," she said.

"Oh, yeah? For how much?"

"The tune of forty-five million dollars."

Kory blinked. "Excuse me?"

"Forty. Five. Million." She said the words slowly and handed him the check.

"What the hell?"

"I tried to give it back, but he wouldn't take it. He refused to take it back. He told me I could donate it to charity if I wanted, but he wasn't going to take it back. And he wrote Tressa off last night."

"This is Tressa's inheritance, Tiff. Her inheritance was forty-five million dollars. The man just gave you his daughter's inheritance."

"Are you serious?"

"Yes!"

"So what should I do first?"

"Head to the bank," he said.

She smiled. "I guess I will."

Epilogue

Boy Crazy premiered shortly after, and Tiffany and Kory arrived in style to the red carpet event for the show. After Tiffany gave her speech she tried to find Kory, but she ran into one of the last people she wanted to see.

"Tiffany, you look amazing," Colby said.

Tiffany couldn't believe he actually showed his face, or that he had the nerve to say two words to her. "You're joking, right?" she asked. She wondered where Kory was because she needed backup. She was going to slap the shit out of Colby.

"Listen, I tried to warn you, but you wouldn't talk to me. I couldn't just leave you a voice mail or text you something so horrible."

"Nope, all you had to tell me was the truth when I asked you in your kitchen, Colby. Before I shared my body with you. Before you recorded me doing something that I thought was special for you. But no harm done. As you can see, it all worked out in my favor. So turn your punk ass around and get the hell outta here!" She saw Kory approaching.

"Listen, Tiffany, I'm so sorry," Colby said.

Kory stepped up. "The lady asked you nicely," he said.

"Oh, you," Colby said and smirked. "Tiffany, tell your li'l boyfriend to fall back."

"You know what, nigga!" Kory drew back and punched him in his face.

Colby went down. He tried to come back, but security was there.

"Miss Richardson, are you okay?" one of the officers asked.

"I'm fine. Please show Mr. Grant to the door," she said.

"This ain't over," he said, wiping the blood from the corner of his lip.

"It doesn't have to be, Colby, just say where!" Kory flexed.

They watched as the security guys forcefully took Colby to the door and made sure he left the premises.

"Nice shot," Tiffany said to Kory.

He straightened his jacket. "I've wanted to do that for months."

"I know. Thanks for coming to my rescue." She gave him a gentle kiss. They went back to the party and danced the rest of the night away. After *Boy Crazy* aired the show quickly rose in rank and Tiffany went from being executive producer of one show to producing four more hit shows on the network.

All was good, and life was good for Tiffany and Kory, but Tressa still manage to stir up trouble when she could. When word got to her about Tiffany receiving her inheritance, she swore that she'd find a way to make her pay. She vowed she'd do whatever it took to make sure Tiffany lived as miserably as she would without Kory, her father, and her money.

Author Bio

Anna Black is a native of Chicago and bestselling author of the *Now You Wanna Come Back* series. Her desire to become a published author didn't develop until her late twenties. She didn't take her writing seriously until several close friends and family members encouraged her to go for it. In 2009, Anna became a bestselling author for her debut release, *Now You Wanna Come Back,* within a matter of weeks. She has since released seven novels and several short stories.

This award—winning author currently lives in Texas with her daughter Tyra, and her adorable Yorkie, Jasmine.